WILD STARS

ROCK HIS WORLD
BOOK TWO

EVIE RILEY

Wild Stars
Rock His World, Book Two
Copyright © 2025
Evie Riley
ISBN: 978-1-77357-741-8
978-1-77357-742-5
Published by Naughty Nights Press LLC
Cover Art By Willsin Rowe

CHAPTER 1

DARE

I HATE INTERVIEWS.

I know, I know, no one really *likes* them, but I've never been good with a camera in my face asking me personal questions, despite the fact I perform for people all the time.

My manager, Penny, tells me I'll get better with them over time, that I need to give myself the chance to "acclimate" to everything. That I need to be *confident* in my talent and myself.

But I find it hard to channel the visage of a successful, rich rockstar when I'm still living in a three-bedroom townhouse with my brother and bandmates, and living on ramen and cinnamon rolls. Not in a giant house that magazines do fucking spreads on, like literally *any* of my label mates, or like the owner of this damn Sylvestro mansion.

Thank God, this place will be lit soon enough, though, once I get enough liquor in my system.

If only they actually put a decent amount of alcohol in these fruity drinks they're serving here. Fucking cheap ass motherfuckers.

Richie, my brother and bassist, takes a drag of his joint, the smoke blowing in my face.

I've had at least six drinks thus far, and I still feel like a ball of nerves.

I kind of wish Felix—aka the headliner of the *Pillars of Rock* tour—wasn't such a grumpy Mcgrumpy-pants earlier when I tried to talk to him, but I guess I'd be pissed, too, if my drummer up and left right at the start of rehearsals.

Still, the guy could have been a little nicer. I brought him a drink as a peace offering!

"Can you even smoke that in here?" I ask, sipping my sugary drink.

Seriously, they could've added more tequila to this.

Richie shrugs as Ines mindlessly scrolls his phone while Spike keeps trying—and failing—to flirt with Jinger Holloway.

Seriously, dude, she's not into you even a little bit. Way out of your league.

"No one's said otherwise," Richie replies, blowing a ring of smoke at me.

I wave through it. I've never been much into the whole smoking thing, mostly because I hate the smell of smoke, period.

Which is why I'd much rather down a good drink to relax my nerves, but this shit isn't doing it.

I glance around, wondering if any of my label mates might have something with a little more punch to soothe my brain goblins, when Penny steps into my view.

"Don't even think about it, Wylde," she snaps, as if she can somehow read my mind.

"I wasn't thinking..."

Richie lets out a laugh, and Penny rolls her eyes. "That's obvious."

I scowl as I drain my drink, glaring at her.

Like us, Penny is new blood for Casualty Records. But then again, I guess being the newest act signed to the label, it makes sense we don't have a big shot manager yet, like Felix Hart does, or even Mateo and Hailee Starr. Hell, we're practically one-hit wonders, and I'm dying to release our next song, *Wild Star*, but it's not quite... there yet.

In fact, it's barely there at all, if I'm being honest, which is why I'm so nervous. This tour is huge for us, but if we don't come up with something soon...

Well, I don't want to think about what could happen, not just to me, but to the rest of my bandmates, if we don't knock our next release out of the park.

"All right, boys, it's show time," Penny states as she straightens my collar, wiping the corners of my mouth with her thumb like I'm a five-year-old.

I swat at her playfully, but she remains stoic and focused, like I'm giving a presidential speech instead of saying a *few* choice words about our tour and where everyone can buy tickets.

Her hazel eyes peer at me from over her over-sized round glasses, and with her dark hair, thick with red streaks and feathers, she looks like a deranged librarian.

How the hell she ended up with a job managing Heart Killer is beyond me, but I'll take her over pink-faced Lou any day.

At least she has good tits.

Richie puts out his joint in the nearest potted plant as Ines and Spike come to line up next to me. Penny gets us lined up and ready while we watch the press settle.

My nerves are frayed, and knowing I have to talk to people only makes me more anxious, but I don't have time to focus on my flipping stomach, or my dry throat, not when the host announces my name.

Fuck me.

THE ROOM IS SPINNING, but that is the way I like it.

At least when the world is moving, I feel still.

Though I keep running over my dumb fucking speech, or lack thereof.

It was like the tiny creatures who run my brain left my body completely. Thank God

Richie stepped in and smoothed everything over, but the damage was already done.

I'd made a damn ass of myself, and I made my band look like a bunch of fucking idiots.

But if there's one thing I *do* know about bad press, it only lasts so long until the next awful water cooler event comes along.

Which is probably why I thought getting wasted and dancing on the kitchen table in the Sylvestro mansion was a good idea ten minutes ago, but now, as my stomach throws a party of its own, I'm wondering if it really was.

I jump down from the table, nearly taking out Jinger, who has the audacity to complain. I can hear Spike, but I can't discern what he's saying, and instead, I wave him off, grumbling to him as I go in search of a bathroom to puke my guts out.

I really shouldn't have had that last drink, or whatever it was that Jinger gave me after my disaster interview.

Or the spoonful of caviar Ines dared me to eat. It tasted gross as fuck.

I cling to the banister, the bright lights of the chandelier making my vision blur. I blindly walk along the hall, shielding my eyes from the overhead light, feeling for a door.

When I arrived earlier, I scoped out the place first, so I know I have to be close to a bathroom.

My hand settles on a knob, and I all but fall into the space, onto plush carpet.

Not a bathroom, but this carpet is soft...

"What the actual fuck?" a steely, gravelly voice cuts through my brain fog as I curl into the carpet, stroking the fibers between my fingers.

I look up to see none other than Mateo Starr, one half of my favorite band, *Mage Of Mercy*.

Like Felix, Mateo is one of the top artists on the label, despite having been on a musical hiatus for the last five years.

But he's *way* hotter than Felix...

Dark gray-blue eyes stare at me as some strands of dark brown hair fall in his eyes haphazardly. Combined with his perfectly shaped lips, impeccable jawline, and his damn near perfect muscles with those badass star tattoos, he's a fucking twenty on a scale of one to ten.

A halo of light erupts around his head, and I swear, I can see cartoon angels and demons jumping around on his shoulders.

"Heyyy Matty..." I slur.

He frowns at me as he nudges me in the side. "What the fuck did you take?" he asks, his voice a deep growl. "And don't call me Matty."

I pet the carpet, stroking its soft, plush fibers as I try to bury myself in it. It doesn't smell as pretty as it looks and I wrinkle my nose.

"I... don't... uh... I had some dr... drinks, and then J... Jinger..."

"Fucking Jinger," he growls as he nudges me in my stomach. "Get up," he orders, and every bone in my body feels like it turns to mush.

I look up at him, his dark hair hanging in his steely gray-blue eyes. He looks like a fucking demon.

A demon with immaculately defined biceps that sports constellation tattoos that make the veins in his arms stand out all the more.

I grew up with this guy's posters on my wall...
Fuuuck he's so much hotter in person.

"Soft..." I murmur as I rub my face in the damn carpet, and then I feel it.

The distinct impulse.

Before I can even grasp what's happening, strong arms pick me up. My legs wobble as an arm settles around my waist—which definitely isn't as trim as Matty's. His fingers sink into my squishy flesh beneath my shirt, and he pushes me forward.

"Move your fucking legs, Dare. Christ."

Matty's voice is deep and sexy.

Like Batman.

I don't know what he's going on about. I can't even feel my fucking legs, but what I can feel is the onset of a heave coming, and the sweats.

Fuck.

My entire body collapses on the ground and Matty curses behind me.

I wretch uncontrollably into a trash can thrust into my face. My vision blurs as I vomit my entire night up.

I fall back when I'm done, on a cold, hard floor. I notice it is no longer carpet, but tile. White, pristine, marble.

I groan as I stare at the ceiling, at the bright white light, catching my breath.

Matty's dark voice cursing me is the last thing I hear.

CHAPTER 2

MATEO

PRESS IS the bane of my existence, but then again, I might be salty because I've been fielding it for the last year since my break up with my ex, Edward Haverish. Who just so happens to be Hollywood's favorite actor at the moment.

Not that Edward doesn't deserve his successes, but his rising stardom only sours my fucking life.

Seriously, every interview I manage to do, they find some way to bring up the fact Edward is starring in some fucking movie or has been photographed with some fucking guy who's got two dicks and a front-row seat to Paris Fashion Week or some shit, all the while smugly waiting for me to crumble into a million pieces.

Fucking idiots.

But even I know how to turn on my charm and stare those fuckers in the face and tell Edward and everyone else about my epic tour and my recent cover with Rolling Stone, or my current number one hit, *Satellites,* which is well on its way to holding its number one spot for the fifth week in a row! After a hiatus of five fucking years!

But no one will even remember my accomplishments carefully pinpointed at tonight's press junket, because Dare fucking Wylde had to have a damn stroke while trying to give a semblance of an interview, and then go on to live out his *Coyote Ugly* dreams in Luciano Sylvestro's kitchen like this event was nothing more than a damn kegger in the woods.

And now he's upchucking his insides violently, and I am more than annoyed.

I am pissed.

I had retired to Luciano's observatory to get

away from the drudgery of dumbass reporters who want to shove my ex's latest gold star down my throat, so I could drink and wallow in solitude and do the one thing that makes me feel less alone.

Stargaze.

Luciano's got an amazing observatory, one that puts mine to shame. I figured I could give my speech, slip away to do some stargazing, and no one would miss me.

At least, not with Hailee around. My sister could do the social thing.

Besides, the press likes her better. She's younger, prettier. More palatable.

If it wasn't for her, you wouldn't even have a comeback.

But I couldn't even salvage a few moments to myself, because Dare stumbled into the observatory, like a newborn lamb, and I didn't think. I just... reacted.

Which I *never* do.

Other people and their bad choices aren't my problem.

Well, not unless we've signed an NDA and agreed on safe words, first.

So why did I give a shit about the Jolly Green Giant all of a sudden?

I grit my teeth, trying to ignore the stench of puke as I gather his thick, dark hair in my fist, holding it back to keep from getting in the way of the repercussions of said bad choices.

Dare groans, and I almost feel bad for the kid.

Because at seventeen years my junior, that's what anyone under the age of twenty-five is to me. A kid.

I let go of him like he's made of fire.

No. Absolutely not, Mateo. Now is not the time to play hero. He's fine.

Dare slumps forward, catching his breath, and I take a step back. He doesn't say anything, and neither do I.

Instead, I just stand there like a lunatic watching him run his tattooed knuckles through his wet, dark, shoulder length hair.

"Fucking hell," I curse, fighting the overwhelming desire to help the poor bastard up and find him somewhere to sleep off his poor decision-making.

I turn away, because I know nothing good comes from my need to *fix* people.

I couldn't fix my ex, and I certainly can't fix Dare Wylde.

I reach the door and turn around to see Dare lying on the floor, staring up at the ceiling. The position makes his black tank top scrunch up the sides, showcasing his pale "love handles" as he calls them.

Just because I've been out of the biz for the last five years, doesn't mean I wasn't keeping tabs on Casualty Record's newest talent, or his penchant for giving the worst interviews on the planet.

Seriously, his manager should hire him a coach or something.

I half debate waltzing over to where he lays to fix his shirt. But I don't.

Instead, I take a deep breath, tell myself he's fine, and I leave.

I shut the door softly, sighing as I put one foot in front of the other.

He's fine.

Lost in my thoughts, I nearly run right over Richie, Dare's less annoying brother and *Heart Killer*'s bassist.

Though when I say he's less annoying, I only mean the guy at least has a sliver of a sense of preservation, where Dare is missing that part of his brain, clearly.

Richie is still annoying, with his mop of blond hair, his big blue eyes, and his perpetual "I'm happy to be here" look.

Like they're well-bred golden retrievers and not rising stars in the music business.

"Your brother's in there," I nod toward the bathroom. "If you're looking for him."

Richie's eyebrows furrow with concern.

"I was. Is he—"

"He's fine," I murmur, shooting an angry glare at Richie, whose eyes look more than a little red.

Fuck me.

These damn kids don't know shit about responsibility these days.

I slide my phone out, jumping to speed dial as I look Richie in the eye.

"You live together, right?" I ask, not trying to give away my concern.

Richie nods. "Yeah. Wait, how do you know—"

"I'm calling you both a driver. You will text me when you and your brother are safe at home."

I tap out my text to my driver, who confirms

within seconds that he has another driver lined up and on his way to pick up the kid and his brother, Tweedle Dee.

"I— I don't even have your number..." he drawls.

I sigh in exasperation. Clearly, whatever he's smoked has eaten up some brain cells, too.

"Your phone, jackass," I bite.

Richie scrambles ungracefully for his phone in his pocket as I scowl.

He listens, though I am not surprised.

Most people can't help but obey me when I use my Dom voice.

Not that I want to dominate Richie Wylde or his brother, but sometimes we use what we have to get the result we need.

And right now, I need Richie to make sure his brother makes it home safely.

Lord knows the trouble Dare would get into otherwise.

Richie barely has the phone out in his hand before I tap his screen with mine, transferring my number to him.

His eyes widen as he nods. "Shit, that's cool, I didn't even know you could do that..."

"This isn't a discussion, *Richard.* You will do

as I say, or your manager will hear about this.," I threaten him, though it is an empty threat. But Dare, Richie, and the others in their band are still so green and I haven't exactly been around much, so I can use that to my advantage.

Scare him just a little.

As long as Dare is safe at home, I'll feel better.

God, what is wrong with me?

Why do I give a shit about the kid?

Richie nods as I slide the phone in my pocket.

"Get your brother, and get the fuck out of my sight," I bark, spinning on my heel and leaving him to his devices.

I traverse the steps, seeing my sister down on the landing, smirking.

"What was that about?" she asks, her violet contacts sparkling under the chandelier.

"None of your fucking business. Are you ready? Or do I have to arrange a carriage for you, too?" I snap.

Hailee rolls her eyes. "I could call it an early night. Get a jump on rehearsals tomorrow. This place is totes boring anyway."

I nod in approval. Smart woman.

"Stop talking like a damn teenager. You're

thirty-five," I chastise her, but she only shakes her head.

"You're thirty-nine, Matty. Not eighty. Loosen up a little," she retorts, slipping her arm into the curve of mine.

I scowl at her, but she takes it in stride.

"I am too old for this fucking shit," I say as I gesture around the room. Felix and Duncan McKay—Sullivan Reign's replacement drummer for the tour—look to be locked in deep conversation while Jinger and Geo are dancing so close I'm half certain they're glued together, while various other c-list acts of Casualty Records continue to throw back drinks and act like fools. Grinding on girls, spilling their drinks. All while, the big wigs count their stacks and smoke their dumb cigars.

"Let's get the fuck out of here."

ONCE MY FEET hit the black marble floor of home, I don't bother with much more than getting ready for bed.

Hailee breaks away for her wing—the left wing of the house—without so much as a Good

Night, which I'm sure some would find rude as hell, but I find more than refreshing.

I know I could technically live on my own, in my own mansion. But after my break up, I didn't *want* to be alone. I'd just spent years with Edward, living together, and the very thought of waking up in a house by myself gave me anxiety. It still does.

Thankfully, Hailee and I bought this place when we were just rising stars like Dare and Richie, and she has been occupying the left wing ever since. Plus, the woman knows me better than anyone, so it's a seamless, easy arrangement.

Together, but separate.

I head for my bathroom, if only so I can wash the stink of Dare's bad decisions off my skin, off my brain. The hot water always helps center me when I feel out of sorts. It's not exactly a hot spring in the middle of Iceland during the auroras, but it'll do.

I run my hands through my hair, letting the scent of bergamot and white sage mixed with eucalyptus fill my lungs. I close my eyes for a moment, the heat infiltrating my senses.

When I finally get out of my shower, I can see the text notification from Richie that they've made it home. I breathe a sigh of relief as I towel dry my hair and slip into a pair of silky, tight briefs, and make my way to my bed.

In all the years I'd been with Edward, I never brought him in here.

To be honest, I've never brought *anyone* into my inner sanctum.

I always said it was because I didn't want any residual energies lingering in my space. I like having my privacy, and I like having things that are just for me. Edward never understood that, even after I moved into his posh home in the valley.

But tonight, as I look at the oversized California King that is nested in the middle of a room full of windows—there is a skylight ceiling and the entire room is made up of floor to ceiling windows—I can't help but feel a sting of sadness.

The stars shine bright, like they always do, as I lie down in the plush blankets, staring up at the sky, but I don't feel less alone like I usually do.

Just once I wish I could share *this...* with someone else.

My chest tightens as I swallow down my sudden emotional thoughts. I shake my head as I get comfortable with the array of pillows and soft bedding, trying not to focus on the chill that comes from sleeping alone.

"You just need a good night's sleep, that's all," I tell myself.

The silence around me is heavy as I curl into my blankets and pillow, alone, closing my eyes.

I let the darkness pull me under.

CHAPTER 3

Dare

My fucking head... Ow.

I groan as light filters in through the bedroom window, my head aching something fierce.

"Rise and shine, boys," Penny chirps and the sound of clinking hooks echoes like a damn loudspeaker in my brain as she pushes the curtains open all around the room.

Richie groans across the room, and I can hear Spike and Ines across the hall cursing as they fight over the bathroom.

"Five more minutes, Penny..." I grumble as I cover my face with my pillow.

Penny kicks me—in my ass—with her heeled boot, which is enough to make me jump out of my fucking skin.

"Five minutes, my ass," she bites as she gives my ass another shove.

I groan, attempting to throw my pillow at her, but my aim is shit and from the huff I hear five feet away, I guess it hits Richie instead.

"She's right," Richie deadpans, and I can hear the annoyance in his voice.

I don't care how right anyone is, I want to stay right fucking here in this damn bed. It's soft, warm, and I feel like I was hit by a damn truck.

I wipe my eyes, groaning as I remember vaguely the events of my previous night. Though it's all a bit of a weird blur, I can remember dancing on the kitchen table, and I remember being carried by strong, sturdy arms...

My face heats as I remember a deep, dark voice nipping at me to move my legs, fingers digging into my sides.

Batman...

No...

Mateo Starr...

I groan as I realize I must've looked like an absolute idiot in front of him.

Mage Of Mercy is still by far one of the most unique sounding progressive rock bands in Hollywood. Shit, I've been a fan of Mateo's act since I was in middle school!

He's the whole reason I even *wanted* to sign to Casualty Records in the first place!

I throw my legs over the side of the bed, flashing my gaze up at Penny, who has the audacity to look at me like I'm nothing more than a child. Her eyebrow raised, arms crossed, she bites, "Get your shit together, Darren. Rehearsal is in an hour."

I hate it when she uses my real name. It's like when your mother yells at you.

And with that, she leaves Richie and me to our devices.

The cold water on my skin helps to wake me up, but it does jack shit for my fucking hangover. I feel like I'll have this headache for eternity at this point.

Seriously, what the fuck did Jinger give me? I'm never doing whatever that was again. Fuck...

I close my eyes for a brief moment, bracing myself against the cold tile. Hazy memories infiltrate my senses, of deep, dark eyes staring down at me, of perfect, exquisitely defined features. Like a Greek god or some shit, mixed with the sight of a night sky.

Despite my hangover and my overall feeling like shit, my cock seems to not be affected as much.

Absentmindedly, I let my hands wander, finding my shaft and relishing in the feel of my own touch. After all, it's part of my morning routine.

Despite what the gossip and rumors about me say, no one but me has serviced this cock in at least a year and a half.

I might be the frontman of *Heart Killer*, but Richie and Spike are the pussy magnets.

You'd think being the token bisexual of the group, I'd have more options, but that's not the case.

I know most dudes want a guy with a six-pack and a loaded wallet, and I have neither.

At best, I've got a body built by cinnamon rolls and a wallet that nowhere near reflects the amount of success someone like Mateo Starr does.

The band's only been with Casualty Records

for a little over a year. We're still trying to find our footing, and while we're more than lucky to be signed to such a fantastic label, we're the new kids, and therefore, we don't get as much attention, or money. Yet.

I try not to think about the truth, for fear of losing my erection.

Instead, I lose myself in thoughts of dark eyes, perfect lips...

I mean, Matty is fucking hot, and I'm pretty sure I'm not the only man in the world who's jacked off to the thought of the guy.

It doesn't mean I like *him*.

I don't even know him.

Not to mention in the limited memory I have, he was kind of being a dick.

Still, all thoughts of bitter Batman aside, it doesn't take long for me to come. I've gotten pretty good at pleasing myself this past year. A few strokes and thrusts while I think about those perfect lips, and I'm over the finish line pretty quick.

A part of me worries I'll never actually find someone, like in the stupid songs about fairytale-written love sense, and the other part of me worries that when I do, they won't live up to my unrealistic expectations, or I just won't be satisfied.

Damned if I do, damned if I don't.

So, for the time being, I just focus on doing what feels good, what feels right, and continue to write about, hopefully, finding someone someday who can handle all of me.

I PILE into the red Malibu with Richie. Spike and Ines speed off on their bikes, while Penny utilizes every Uber or Lyft she can and bills the label. I know we could do the same, but there's something genuine about staying true to our roots. Richie bought the car with our first advance, and it's as much mine as it is his.

But he's a way better driver than I am, so I don't fight him when he plops into the driver's seat every time.

Within seconds, we're speeding off toward the highway as I poke around the radio stations, finally stopping when I settle on a station playing *Mage Of Mercy*'s newest hit, *Satellites*.

"I'll fly across space and time, baby, if it would only make you mine. I'll fight the asteroids, dispel the meteorites, baby, nothing can keep me away from my... my satellite..."

Matty's deep vocals are like smooth, black velvet. My brain turns to mush a little as he breathlessly sings his words, and my cock twitches.

Nonchalantly, I adjust myself as I let out an agitated sigh.

"That was *Mage Of Mercy* with *Satellites*. God, it's so good to have new music from Mateo and Hailee Starr again, don't you agree Tiffany?"

I roll my eyes as Richie speaks up.

"Something wrong?" he asks, and I glance at him from my seat.

I curl my legs up, wrapping my arms around them. I hate sitting like a normal person, it feels uncomfortable.

Memories of Matty's dark Batman voice reverberate in my brain. His authoritative tone, his bite.

I purse my lips.

First chance meeting my idol and I fucking blew it.

And all the contents of my stomach, no less.

Fuck, I'm hungry.

"You ever meet someone you admire and immediately regret it?" I murmur.

Richie sighs. "Does this have anything to do with Mateo Starr?" he asks.

I furrow my eyebrows. "How did you—"

"He called us a car last night, *insisted* I make sure you got home safe. Even made me fucking text him like he was my dad or some shit."

I blink as I try to remember the events of last night clearly, but I didn't remember Mateo doing anything like that.

All I can remember is me throwing up and him yelling at me and pushing me around.

"Yeah, well, I'm sure he would have done the same for anyone else." I shrug.

Richie purses his lips, returning his gaze to the road. "You ever just... wish you could go back in time and do shit over?" he asks.

"Yeah, kinda feel that way right about now," I whine as I rub my temples. "You think Penn has any Advil at the studio? My brain hurts."

Richie shakes his head. "That's why I stick to fucking weed, man. The natural shit. Never leaves me feeling like garbage."

I bang my head against the window, nonchalantly flipping him off.

"Fuck you," I bite as I close my eyes and let the motion of the drive lull me into a half sleep.

When we finally arrive at the studio, I feel a little better, and my headache has started to subside, but I'm still dragging ass. Thankfully, the studio is posh as shit and they have, like, the best break room I've ever seen.

Seriously, their collection of K-Cups and super fancy drinks is a huge motivator.

Richie takes off for the rehearsal studio, but I keep walking.

"Where are you—"

"Caffeine and sustenance, man. If I don't eat something or get some fucking coffee in my system, I think I *will* perish," I tell him.

Richie only rolls his eyes, but waves me off. "Fine. But that caramel cappuccino shit *isn't* actually coffee, you know!" he yells as I make a beeline for the break room, running headfirst into something large and solid.

No, not something, *someone*.

"Jesus Christ, Dare, are you still drunk?" a bitter voice beckons.

I look up with wide, surprised eyes.

"Oh shit, Matty, I'm sorry, I—"

"Don't fucking call me that," he nips as he shifts his stance in the doorway.

I look around him to see the spread of pastries and muffins on the counter, and my stomach growls.

"I'm sorry, just a little hungry, and—" I bumble like a fucking idiot, then blurt, "Felix calls you Matty."

Mateo scowls. "Felix is annoying at best. I don't pay any attention to what that asshole does."

I swallow harshly as I reply, "Noted."

Just as he moves to leave, I stop him.

"Hey, um... Richie told me you, uh... what I mean is, uh..."

Matty raises a sharp eyebrow, his expression a blend of stoic and annoyed. "English, please, Dare."

The way he says my name makes a shiver run up my fucking spine.

It's smooth and warm, like caramel cappuccino.

I blink furiously, trying to keep focused on being polite and thanking the man for making sure I was okay, and not focusing on the sexy way he says my name.

Which makes my ADD riddled brain burst with thoughts that are probably way too inappropriate for the workplace.

I fight the heat that wants to rush into my cheeks as I hold his steely gaze.

You can do this! He's just a guy.

Yeah, a guy you totally had posters of in your room as a teenager.

Who happens to be way hotter in person than in your dreams.

"I just wanted to say thanks. For, uh… helping me out last night."

For holding my hair back and letting me make a legit mess of myself in front of you, Sir.

Where the fuck did that come from?

Something shifts in Matty's eyes and his expression softens only a little.

"Yes, well, someone clearly needed to." He grinds his jaw.

What is his problem?

Why am I so hot all of a sudden?

"Matty, come on, can you just, like—"

Batman practically shoves me up against the doorframe, and for a moment, I can't even fathom the thought of K-Cups or muffins, because the sight of those perfect lips, that dark gaze, and my stupid fucking twitching cock are all I can focus on.

Matty leans a tattooed arm against the doorframe, his lips curling back to expose perfectly white canines. The veins in his biceps make the constellation lines look alive, and I have to remember to breathe.

Not only because my idol is inches away from me, but because something about his aura is making my brain feel like mush, like when he sings.

I swallow harshly, as he growls, "I said, don't fucking call me that."

And because I truly am a damn idiot with probably only one functioning brain cell at the moment, I don't shut up like I should.

No, my last kamikaze brain cell feels like *fighting*.

I challenge his space, gazing down his fiery pupils as I respond, "You aren't the fucking boss of me, *Matty*." I smile smugly as I purposefully enunciate his name, using my size to shove him back against the side of the doorframe, and steamroll my way into the break room.

"Ungrateful little shit. Next time I'll let you fucking rot," he snaps, and with that, Mateo

Starr leaves me to question every decision I've made in the last twenty-four hours.

"Fuck," I breathe once he's out of sight. "What the hell is wrong with me today?" I run my hand through my hair as I wait with bated breath for my caramel cappuccino.

"Whatever, Dare. Just grab your coffee and put Sexy Batman out of your brain," I tell myself as I grab my drink and head off the studio.

CHAPTER 4

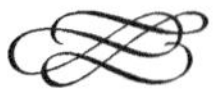

MATEO

GET A HOLD OF YOURSELF.

I run my hand over my face as I try to regain my sense of self.

Because, for a brief moment—when Dare *brattily* tried to shove *me* against the doorframe —I nearly forgot who I was and where we were.

My vision went red at the bite of his defiance, making my damn heart stop, and my breath catch.

The desire to put this damn kid in fucking time out made my palms and my cock twitch.

And then he had the balls to get in *my* space?

Oh, hell fucking no.

If anything, Dare's attitude should piss me off, and to be fair, it does.

But it also is so fucking tempting.

I bet he'd submit beautifully under my hand...

What the fuck? Where did that come from?

I shove off the wildly inappropriate thoughts.

Maybe I'm just out of it because I had a rough night.

After all, I was up on and off because I just couldn't get comfortable.

And then Dare had to nearly knock me over and act like a shy, sweet little thing, pulling me in with big puppy dog eyes, only to lash out and bite me.

And the most annoying part of all of that is that I ate it up like fucking candy.

Yeah, clearly a lack of sleep is throwing me off my game.

I open the door to the studio, deciding to leave Dare Wylde and his *Heart Killer* buddies to their own devices and instead focus on the main goal; the damn show.

Hailee is perched on a chair in the corner, scrolling on her phone absentmindedly. She barely gives me a nod as I walk in.

"Come on, let's get this shit going," I bite.

Hailee rolls her eyes. "You're in a mood today," she replies.

"If it matters, I didn't get a whole lot of sleep last night, and then I ran into that stupid kid..."

Hailee sets her phone down as she heads for her spot behind her keyboard. "What kid?"

I grab my guitar, slinging the strap over my shoulder. "Fucking Dare Wylde."

Hailee raises an eyebrow. "Richie's brother?"

It's my turn to look at her with surprise. "Yeah, you know them?"

Something shifts in her eyes, but I don't have a moment to grasp it as she tunes her keyboard.

"I mean, sort of. I've seen them at events and stuff, but I don't, like, know them know them, ya know," she says carefully.

"But from what I've seen... they both seem... nice. Fun. Not completely ruined by fame, yet."

I strum the strings on my guitar, making sure to tune my instrument properly just as Helena Howler, our current manager, walks in.

Since Drew Axel of *Axe 2 Grind* is on a hiatus or whatever, and our regular manager, Bridget, is out on maternity leave, Howler offered to step in for the duration of the *Pillars of Rock* tour.

"They are children, Hailee. Stupid kids who don't know what the fuck they are doing. They're an accident waiting to happen."

Hailee shakes her head. "Richie is twenty-six and Dare is twenty-three, so I'm pretty sure that makes them adults," she defends, which only irritates my nerves more.

Why is she sticking up for them?

We're supposed to be old and grumpy and judgey together!

"Twenties? That's barely out of fucking high school, Hailee."

"You know, I think living in the fucking mountains doing all that yoga rotted your brain," she teases, tucking some dark curls behind her ear.

"It wasn't *yoga*, it was *tantra*," I correct her.

"Whatever. Depriving yourself of happiness and pleasure is only going to make you fucking miserable, clearly. Maybe *you* could learn a thing or two from the *kids*," she nips, adding in a sarcastic, "Or perhaps you just need to get fucked."

I make the final adjustment on my guitar as Helena calls over the loud speaker, cutting me off from spewing venom at my pain in the ass sister.

What is *her* problem today?

"All right, guys, show me what ya got," Howler calls out, popping her bubblegum.

"With pleasure, Howler." I strum the first few notes of *Satellites*.

Despite our room being mostly sound-proof, I can still *hear* noise carrying from down the hall on the other side of us. Noise that sounds a lot like electric guitars and heavy drums.

"What the fuck is that?" I snap.

"What?" Hailee asks as Helena presses the button again.

"Don't tell me you can't hear that shit." I huff as Helena narrows her gaze at me. I gesture to the door before I open it slightly.

"What are you talking about?" she asks.

"I can feel the fucking bass from down the hall."

Hailee groans. "It's probably just *Heart Killer* warming up. No big. The studio is bound to be packed today, since we're all here rehearsing. Play your shit and drown it out."

I shoot her a glare. If only it were that simple, but Hailee of all people knows I can't play if I can't *concentrate.* And I can't concentrate with *Heart Killer* wailing down the hall like a bunch of dying cats.

I need order in my life; without it things are utter chaos. And I can't handle chaos.

Attempting to heed her advice, I try to block out the faint sounds of *Heart Killer* down the hall, but just as I strum my guitar once more, I hear the clash of cymbals and a loud wail of guitar. Again.

I glare at Hailee, who throws her hands up in the air.

I slide my guitar off of myself as I head for the door.

"Mateo... come on..." my sister whines as Howler tries to call me back in, but I flip both of them off.

This is what I mean about stupid kids. They don't have any respect for anyone but themselves, and even that is in poor amount.

I can handle Dare being a stupid ass at a party, but it's another thing to come into my job and cause me chaos where I absolutely don't fucking need it.

As I traverse down the hall, the music gets louder; wailing electric guitars and heavy drums are accompanied by Dare's sultry voice.

It's an odd combination of dark and operatic tinged with an almost eighties metal sound.

I have to admit, I've never heard anything like it. But I don't have time to focus on the talents of Dare and his band.

I throw open the door to their room, to see Penny and Palo turn around in surprise.

Dare keeps playing and singing, his head bent over so his dark black hair falls in his face.

Combined with his thick, tattooed arms and his frayed jeans, he looks every bit like the grunge high school rock kid.

"Mateo, what—" Penny stammers as I brush past her to press the com button.

"Do you not know the definition of the word, *soundproof,* Dare?"

Dare curses as he looks up, stopping his playing while the rest of the band ceases as well.

On the other side of the studio room, I can see the back door is cracked open by a quarter.

"Excuse me?" he says, cocking his head to the side.

I press the button again. "I can hear your dying cat all the way down the fucking hall. Some of us are trying to work here."

Hailee's footsteps enter the room as Dare all but throws down his guitar, heading for the door that separates the engineering room from the studio.

His cheeks are pink and his dark eyes are full of fire, his jaw tense.

He runs a hand through his shiny, jet black hair as he comes up to my chest, staring up at me like I'm the school bully who has just taken his lunch money.

My entire body heats and the overwhelming desire to put him in his place is like a compulsion I don't *want* to deny, but I know I have to.

"I have been rehearsing in this studio for over a week and no one has complained I'm too fucking loud."

"Clearly Felix and Geo are deaf," I bite.

Dare huffs, and the sight reminds me of an angry kitten.

It's almost *cute* or endearing.

Almost.

"You have a lot of nerve coming into *my* studio and interrupting *my* rehearsal," he argues.

Richie is beside him in a flash and I feel Hailee's nails on my side, squeezing.

Telling me to back down.

Dare brushes his chest against me, challenging my gaze. We're both nearly the same height, except for the fact I've got at least four inches on the man, which is saying something considering I'm six foot four, but despite his softer shape, he's got a bit of force behind his build. Though I'd garner a wager that Dare doesn't use his body—or treat it—the way he should.

Not like I would.

Where the fuck did that thought come from?

Angered by Dare's *distraction*, I push back against his chest.

"Perhaps I shall whine and whimper at high pitched frequencies and then *you* will understand true interruption."

Dare stares me down.

"Music too loud for you, old man?" he snickers. "Maybe you should find a drum circle instead and complain to them. Now, if you're done, I have a show to rehearse for."

My palm twitches and my fingers *itch* to wrap themselves around his throat.

How dare he!

I'm still under fucking forty for another month at least!

"Okay, come on, big guy..." Howler pulls me back, just as Richie attempts to grab Dare.

Dare shrugs him off, snapping away from me as he heads through the open door, slamming it.

The room is quiet, so quiet the only sound that can be heard is the steady breathing of *Heart Killer*'s remaining members.

"Well, now, that wasn't so hard, was it?" I bark as I push away from Hailee and Howler, heading down the hall.

When I get to my studio, it's quiet, and I can finally concentrate.

Hailee walks in, glaring at me. "You didn't have to be such a tyrant," she says calmly.

I sling my guitar over my shoulder. "If you're nice, people walk all over you," I reply, my voice even and cold. "If you want respect, you must demand it." Anger is flooding me like a drug. It makes me want to fucking punch something.

I hate feeling out of control.

How is it that one dumb kid can make me feel so, so...

Powerless?

Hailee's eyes glisten, and she purses her lips. "Right. Because earning it is so fucking last season, right?" she says, just as Helena pushes the button once more.

"Hailee... it's not..."

"Whatever, Mateo. Forget about it, let's just focus on the music, yeah?" She lets out a loud sigh, brushing some highlighted hair over her shoulder.

"Start with Satellites," Howler orders, her voice unwavering. Pulling me back to the task at hand.

Hailee plays the opening notes and I sing.

"I've been all across the galaxy, searching for a sign..." My hands shake, and I feel like shit. But I don't have time to think about Dare and his bratty attitude, or his solid weight against me.

Or Hailee's words that cut to me the bone.

I don't have time to think about the chaos. I need to be in control.

"Searching like a lost ship, searching for my satellite."

Hailee's soft vocals filter in over mine as she

sings, "I need a satellite, to anchor me, call me home."

I glance at her, and the softness in her expression makes me feel even worse.

I strum out the chords, losing myself in my lyrics once more.

"Can you hear me? I'm calling satellite, satellite. Bring me home."

CHAPTER 5

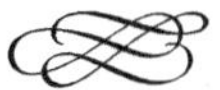

DARE

I POWER-WALK DOWN THE HALL, heading straight to the breakroom.

What is Matty's problem anyway?

I've never had an issue rehearsing here, over the last year I've been here!

I make my way to the Keurig, fixing for another cup of caramel cappuccino to soothe my frayed nerves.

I don't know what came over me, either. Normally, I'm not so easily pissed off, but something about Matty's venomous tone and the way he got in *my* face... like, flipped a fucking switch or something.

I'm not an argumentative person in general. I avoid conflict at all costs, ninety-nine percent of the time.

So why did I feel like *fighting* with Mateo Starr was a good idea?

Why on God's green earth did I think pushing his fucking buttons was a good idea?

Because watching the man's pupils dilate like that makes me feel powerful.

God, am I really that *fucked up?*

I run my hand over my face as I try to dispel the memory of Matty and his pretty mouth, of the way he clenched his jaw when I got in his face.

Of the fucking hardness growing in my pants as I *think* about getting in his face.

I adjust my stupid cock with a grunt.

Yeah, that's never going to happen even if the guy likes guys.

He doesn't like you one fucking bit.

I'm not obtuse, I know Matty's break up with Edward Haverish was highly publicized, and Eddy Spaghetti is on track to win a fucking

Oscar, but that's not *my* problem, and that's no excuse to be a dick.

Someone should give that asshole a good spanking and set him right.

Immediately, the goblins that run my brain latch onto the idea of Mateo Starr, bare-assed with my fucking handprint glowing red on his cheeks, and my cock twitches.

Fucking ay! Now is not the time for dumb ass fantasies!

I twist the coffee carousel and pluck my K-cup from the line-up and pop it in the Keurig to try and get my mind—and my cock—back in order.

The machine whirrs as it heats up, and I brace my hands against the counter as I suck in a deep breath, letting it out slowly, if only to try and calm my frayed nerves.

I need to *focus*. I need to get this damn coffee–not coffee, and I need to get back to work.

Usually, I check the doors before we start jamming, but I have to admit, this morning I am just not myself. That's fucking clear as a bell.

Richie knocks, even though the door is open, pulling my attention.

"Hey," he says cautiously.

"Hey," I reply as I grab a rice crispy treat from the basket while I wait for my coffee-not coffee.

"What was that about?" he asks as he slowly approaches me, sliding his hands in his pockets.

"Honestly... I don't fucking know. I'm just a goddamn mess today, Rich."

Richie leans against the counter next to me, chewing on his lip. "We all have bad days, Dare. That doesn't make you an asshole," he says calmly.

"No, but getting in Mateo Starr's fucking face doesn't make me any less of one," I chirp as I tear into the crispy treat. The marshmallowy goodness makes me feel better even if it's short-lived.

Richie smirks. "I'm pretty sure he can handle it. You're probably not the first person to tell him off. Dude is a fucking icebox."

I sigh as I swallow another bite of my emotional support treat. "I should have checked the room better. I should have—"

"Shit happens. Don't sweat it. We're all under pressure for this tour, you know. Not just you."

I look at him from under my lashes, noting his demeanor and body language are unusual, even for him.

My brother is one of the most confident individuals I know, so to see him melancholy makes me do a double take.

"Something bothering *you*?" I grab another crispy treat, offering it to him. "Need to eat your feelings too?"

He pushes it away. "You know that shit is full of sugar and is terrible for you, right?" He flashes me with a half smile.

"I ain't never seen anyone frown while eating a rice crispy treat," I reply, grinning like an idiot just to make a point.

"Darren...." He shakes his head, but I don't miss the way the corners of his mouth perk up.

"Just saying. One rice crispy treat won't erase your abs overnight."

Richie purses his lips as he grabs the wrapped treat from me and I smile victoriously.

"I'll make a deal with you," Richie offers as he tears open the package.

"What's that?"

"We go back into that studio, we play our fucking asses off, and after? We go out to Fuku for some sushi and drinks with the guys. Kick back, relax a little. Maybe we can get some press out of it," he says with a half-smile.

I chew the last bit of my rice crispy treat, leaving no crumbs.

"Deal." I grab my drink as the machine shuts off, casting my brother a genuine smile. "Thanks, man," I say.

"For what?" Richie asks.

"For always having my back and making me feel like less of an asshole."

Richie's gaze softens. "You're not an asshole, Dare. You're just a fucking brat," he teases as he finishes his treat.

I sip my coffee-not-coffee as he comes up behind me, and we exit the breakroom, heading back to the studio where Ines and Spike look bored as hell as Penny elaborates about something with her hands up in the air.

"You guys ready to get this show on the road?" I ask, pulling their attention.

"Fuck yes," Spike says as he all but jumps out of his seat and heads for his instrument.

Richie takes his place and grabs his bass.

"Take it from the top with *On The Edge*." Penny says authoritatively.

I strum out the first few chords of the song, channeling my best impression of a rockstar, and focus on the music.

And for the moment, that's enough.

CHAPTER 6

Mateo

"It's so nice to go out again, like we used to," Celina says with pouty lips. "I missed this."

Hailee toasts her cosmopolitan with Celina's vodka redbull.

I take a sip of my cocktail, some concoction of Japanese coffee-flavored whiskey and cherry blossom liquor, which is not as sweet as it sounds. Then again, I prefer a strong drink with a bitter bite.

Geo smiles as Hans—Hailee's make up artist—nods in agreement.

"It's nice to see Sleeping Beauty leave his

tower once in a while, too," Geo says with a smirk.

I roll my eyes. "I do things. I'm not a shut in," I bite.

It's true. I do leave my house and studio. I've even got a standing reservation at Saint & Sinner, the newest sex club that opened up.

Hailee appraises me with an annoyed glare, almost as if she can read my mind, and I think maybe that's not as good as it sounds.

It's not like I'm a sex addict or anything, I just... need to relax once in a while.

And my definition of relaxing differs from everyone else's.

"When was the last time you went out with all of us, like this? Seriously. It was before you and Ed broke up."

The air thins as she says his name, and I don't miss the looks that come over everyone's faces. It's like she dropped a bomb in the middle of a table, just by saying his name.

I sigh, knowing there isn't any arguing with her at this point. After all, we broke up a year ago, officially. Contracts ripped up and all...

"Yeah, well, maybe I was trying to figure my shit out, Hailee. I was with the guy for five fucking years. Forgive me if I needed some space."

I drain my drink and push it to the side, capturing the attention of our waitress and beckon her for another.

Celina is the first to speak. She says the words softly, imploring me with her gaze. "Five years is a long time."

Geo bumps my shoulder. "But that's the past. You're doing fucking great *now,* man. Look at you."

I glance at Geo's dark, kind eyes, and the air that settles around us is strangely comforting.

"Your comeback is lit." Geo waggles his eyebrows. "Five weeks in the number one spot, shit. I'll never knock you out at this point," he teasess smoothly.

"It's not a comeback, Geo. It's a glow-up. Obviously." Hans winks. "All that yoga really paid off, huh?" Hans giggles.

I shoot him a dominant glare that makes him shut right the fuck up. "It wasn't yoga," I nip.

Hailee rolls her eyes. "Right, it was tantra." She giggles.

"Yes. And I think maybe you all could learn a

thing or two from the practice of *holding things in,*" I say, taking a swig of my drink.

Geo raises his beer, taking a sip as he laughs. "You've been holding it in long enough, don't you think?"

Celina giggles and Hans shakes his head.

"Indulgence is no longer indulgence if it is routine," I grumble.

Which is why I only watch at Saint & Sinner, and do not engage.

A part of me worries I'll never truly *indulge* in anyone, again.

Not unless I want to suffer a broken heart and soul.

Hailee chimes in. "All I'm saying is it's okay to have a little fun. You're not dead, you know. You just have to remember how to live."

Hans purrs in contentment. "That needs to be on a t-shirt somewhere."

I can't help but shake my head as the waitress drops off my drink and I waste no time taking a sip.

"And indulgence is fine. In moderation," Geo declares as he sets his drink down.

I raise an eyebrow at him. Not that the man

doesn't drink or *indulge* in shit, but it is kind of odd to see it when he does. I guess even angels from Christian rock can fall off the wagon sometimes.

Geo's smile doesn't reach his kind eyes. I don't have many people I consider friends—mostly a lot of acquaintances and assholes who want to be *seen* with me rather than be with me —but I'd go out on a limb and say the straight edge Marilyn Manson looking motherfucker is the closest thing I have to a best friend besides my sister.

And he might be the *only* person at the table who actually knows about my... lifestyle.

I don't like talking about my relationship with Edward, if only because I *can't really* talk about our relationship, due to our NDA.

The one I made him sign as my submissive.

Even though he broke the terms of our contract, the clause was more than iron clad and prevents *both* of us from discussing the details of our relationship publicly.

For this very reason.

No one—except maybe Geo—could ever understand that my heartbreak extended beyond matters of the actual heart. Though, I didn't disclose much else except the fact that it was over and I was leaving the bastard.

Edward broke my *trust.*

More than once.

And I let him do it.

I let him hurt me, because I fucking loved him, and all I was to him, was some kink, some scheduled activity. It wasn't a life with me Edward wanted. It was just... sex to him. Our contract was nothing more than a fucking business proposal.

He made that more than clear, when I found him fucking someone else.

My contract was explicitly clear that while he was under my care, he would abide by my rules, including being *faithful* to me.

I believed when he signed our contract that he took it as seriously as I did.

Because to me, it wasn't just a *kink.* He wasn't just some guy I enjoyed tying up, so I could make him beg for mercy.

He was *mine.*

In every sense of the word.

I don't *do* relationships well, mostly because of my singular preferences. Because relationships to me are not fickle, chaotic things I do on a fucking whim.

I need to know when I am *giving* myself, when I am *serving* my sub, that I can trust them. Words are just that... words.

I write them all the time, and I know they hold no true weight.

Anyone in the world can tell me they love me. And they do. At shows, on social media posts, at the fucking grocery store.

But ink is eternal. It stains the paper with truth that is irrefutable. It's trust in black and white, a promise.

That contract was me handing Edward my heart and soul in ink.

I put my career on hold to focus on him. To serve him.

I handed him my black heart on a silver platter.

I moved into his fucking house, for God's sake, because I thought that was the way things were supposed to go. I thought I'd finally found someone I could settle down with and build a fucking life.

But Edward Haverish makes his own fucking rules, apparently.

I should have split the first time I found him fucking someone else, but I didn't.

Because I stupidly thought as his Dom, I could correct him and his behavior. I could make him bend and see the err of his ways. That I was *worthy* of his attentions.

I thought that I could fix him.

Geo's smile isn't knowing, but it's genuine, and for the moment, that's enough. I guess.

"Holy shit, what are the fucking odds?" Geo says, his voice ticking up an octave as he rises from his chair.

My gaze follows him and the blood immediately drains from my body when I see him wrap his arms around a rather familiar looking individual.

"Hey man!" Dare says with excitement as Richie waves, smiling at my sister and friends.

"Hey Hailee." His smile is stupid and lazy, and it irritates me. Also the way he's looking at my sister is suspicious, but I don't have time to interject when Geo speaks.

"Ya'll should totally join us," he says.

My jaw tightens, as does my grip on my drink.

Dare's gaze catches mine and I see the corners of his lips perk up.

"I'd love to," he says, that bratty undertone to his voice making my blood rush and my cock twitch.

Bad fucking idea.

I do my best to remain apathetic, or at the very least, *appear* apathetic.

It irritates me how just one fucking look from this kid can get my fucking panties in a twist.

Maybe Hailee is right. Maybe I need to get fucked, seriously.

I sip my whiskey drink, glancing away from the little brat.

Hans flags our waitress down as Celina and Hailee busy themselves with dragging extra chairs over, like Fuku is a damn McDonald's and not a high-end restaurant.

Seriously, what is wrong with them?

Dare settles between Geo and I, his frame entering my space.

I know I should move over, but I don't want to give this damn kid an inch. I know he'll take a mile, and I'm not in a giving mood. The past twenty-four hours, it's like I can't get away from him.

"Whatcha drinking, old man?" Dare quips with a grin, nudging me with his elbow.

This close, I can smell the cologne rolling off of him. Some cheap, knock-off crap that probably came off the back of a truck somewhere.

He runs his free hand through his hair, which looks a little shinier than it did earlier, but equally still disheveled and unkempt.

My palm twitches as I watch his fingers slide through the silky locks.

I shouldn't know what that feels like, but I do, and it's all I can think about.

I grip my glass tightly. "Nikka," I bite.

Dare raises an eyebrow. "La Femme Nikita? I didn't know she made drinks."

I roll my eyes, my tongue sharp as the bitterness of my whiskey. "It's Japanese whiskey."

Idiot.

Dare cocks his head to the side, twisting his lips. "Sounds stuffy."

I pause as I bring the drink to my lips. "It's sophisticated."

I savor the taste of the cherry blossom liquor that only heightens the coffee flavoring. The bitterness on my tongue soothes my fractured nerves.

I refuse to move for Dare.

"You wouldn't know anything about that though, would you?" I snark.

Hailee laughs loudly, and I glance across the table to see Richie telling some story that has her, Celina, and even Hans, captivated. Geo smiles at me as he raises his drink.

The waitress drops off a fresh round of drinks, setting a rather sweet looking concoction in front of Dare.

Complete with a toasted marshmallow on top.

"Is that a—"

"S'mores Martini, yeah. Totally sophisticated," Dare says with a grin as he lifts it, popping his pinky.

I scowl at his sarcasm.

After he takes a sip, he sets the glass down, and my cock twitches at the sight of the froth left on his lips.

Don't get any ideas. This one's off limits.

For starters, he's seventeen years younger than me, and he's also irritating and annoying as fuck, even if he does play for both teams.

He blinks absentmindedly, his gaze flashing to my lips. "What?"

I scoff, taking a sip of my drink as he stares at me with marshmallow froth all over his perfect, pink lips.

No. No. No. No!

"You have a little... something on your face," I drawl.

Dare's eyebrows furrow, as he runs his thumb across his lips, smearing the marshmallow more.

Then the fucker has the audacity to open his mouth, and *lick* the cream right off.

My jaw tenses. Right along with my stupid fucking cock.

"Right, Dare?" Richie calls, breaking the weird tension between us.

"Right!" he chimes in excitedly, licking the rest of the froth from his lips quickly, and I shift my position in my seat if only to quell my unruly fucking dick that seems to have a mind of its own.

I watch intently as Dare and Richie tell their stories, and everyone at the table bursts into fits of laughter over their sordid tales of exploring the rabbit holes of Hollywood.

In some ways, I envy the ease they have of flitting from place to place, not giving two shits about how or where they'll end up.

I've never been so carefree. Everything I've ever done has been calculated.

I've left nothing in my life to chance. I wouldn't be where I am—a top selling musician with a wall full of awards—if I had serendipitously left it all up to fate.

Dare animatedly tells his stories, bumping into me without warning, nearly knocking me over. Several times. I'm not convinced he isn't doing it on purpose, but I do not yield, nor will I ever yield for this fucking kid.

It'll be a cold day in hell.

After the third drink, I think social hour is finally over, and we rise to leave.

"We should totally keep this party going," Richie suggests charismatically.

Hans animatedly jumps up and down with Celina. "Oh my God, yasssss we totally should!" he says.

I roll my eyes as I look at Geo, imploring him to put an end to this shit. It's nearing eight pm already, we've been at this damn joint for like three hours.

But Geo only grins wickedly at me as he nods. "Absolutely! I haven't had this much fun in ages!"

I'm going to kill him.

Hailee loops her arm in mine, gazing up at me with glassy eyes. "Oh, come on, don't be a party pooper." She pouts.

I glance at Dare, who is bouncing on his black glam heeled boots like a child with a stupid ass grin on his face.

"Yeah, Matty... don't be a fucking party pooper." He pouts, taunting me. The corners of my eyes and mouth twitch along with my palm.

Hailee casually whispers to me, "Come on, live a little. You deserve to have a good time. Let Edward see you *thriving* when you're plastered on page six. Living your best life *without* him."

I sigh as I look down at my sister, and I know I'm going to pay for this later.

I glance at Richie and Dare.

"What did you have in mind?"

DARE

I HAVE TO ADMIT, I am not one hundred percent certain that we'll *actually* get into Saint & Sinner tonight, but it's worth a shot, right?

Fake it 'til you make it and all that?

"Oh, I've never been to S&S!" Hailee giggles. "I've been dying to go."

"Don't you need, like, a reservation?" Hans asks.

Shit, I hadn't thought of that.

"I can get us in," Matty says in his sexy Batman voice, pulling all of our attention.

"Uh… since when do you go clubbing?" Celina asks, raising an eyebrow.

I watch as Matty shrugs, his expression stoic as usual.

"I've been there once or twice," he replies, shifting his stance.

Hailee shifts closer to my brother with a grin. "Now we *have* to go. I have to see my brother actually act like a rockstar for once and get us into a damn strip club."

Matty rolls his eyes before glancing at me. "It's not a strip club, Hailee. It's a sex club. There is a difference."

"As long as they have drinks and ass, I'm in," I chime with excitement.

Richie clears his throat as he looks at me, raising an eyebrow, and I realize before he even speaks what he's implying.

Fuck, that means I'm going to have to call a damn Uber.

"I, uh… guess I'll call an Uber and meet you guys there…" I say, shooting some finger guns at my brother, if only to not look like a complete asshole.

Though I wish just for once I was the one who could drive the car around with a hot date.

Matty's hand enters my vision as he pushes my phone down.

I glance up at him, biting my damp lip as I try to remember this asshole is actually, an asshole and not some prince charming in a black silk button down and tight leather pants.

"No need, I'll have my driver get us," he says sternly as Celina and Hans echo their excitement.

"Oh, uh... thanks. I guess," I grumble.

Matty suavely pulls out his phone, and in a very Bruce Wayne fashion, calls us a fucking limousine.

I swear the thing barely takes five minutes to arrive, just as Hailee and Richie disappear around the corner.

The four of us crawl in, and I can't help but marvel at the space in this thing. I swear, it's the nicest limo I've ever been in.

Way better than the limo I rented with Richie for prom. Which I went to dateless, of course.

I guess I couldn't blame anyone because I looked like a fucking blue penguin from Super Mario in my powder blue tux.

"Shit, this is nice," I say as I find my seat.

Hans and Celina seem to make themselves at home, diving into the cooler immediately.

Matty slides in the seat next to me, leaving ample space between us. "Figured you'd like it," he says calmly.

My eyebrows furrow in confusion. "What?"

"That's what you want, right? To be *seen* like a big bad rockstar?"

Something about his words feels harsh, but beneath them is something else.

Sadness, I think.

"No, I—"

Matty crosses his legs as Hans and Celina take selfies. It's like they are in their own little world, completely oblivious to us.

"I just... don't want to be irrelevant, you know." I shift my position, feeling strangely warm.

"You're not irrelevant, Dare."

The three marshmallow martinis must have gone to my head, because I shift a little closer, sighing with disdain.

Sometimes, being cheerful is a fucking chore when you're truly depressed.

"Yes, I am," I mumble, looking toward the tinted window on the other side. "I'm a one hit wonder. If I can't come up with another hit, that is..."

God, what did they put in those fucking martinis?

Matty sighs beside me. "Writer's block?" he asks, his voice smooth, like velvet.

I don't look at him. I keep my gaze trained on the city that flashes by. If I don't look at him, I can pretend that maybe I am not a fucking idiot.

"More like cock block, but then again..." I whistle. "I just want to write a song that's not about *wanting* something you can't have, you know? I want to write a song about being fucking in it."

"Then be *in it,* Dare. You're young, probably have a fuck ton of people just begging to fuck you and get a song written about them. That's like rockstar 101."

I sigh, crossing my legs. "Yeah, well, I don't, okay..." I turn to flash him a glare, only to realize he's a lot closer than he was before.

Something about that makes my blood rush, and my damn cock twitch.

Matty cocks his head to the side, appraising me with a calculating gaze. "Is that why you have such an attitude? Need to get laid?"

I scoff at him, my cheeks flushing at his insinuation. "I do not have an attitude, Matty." I grin when the vein over his left eye twitches. "And getting laid is Richie's talent, not mine."

Mateo's lips twitch, and I realize all at once I put my foot in my fucking mouth, because his *sister* is off probably getting her clit sucked by my brother at this very moment.

I mean, I saw the way she was clinging to him like a bee on honey, Christ. Not to mention he's been smitten with her since they got handsy at the mansion the other night.

Why that little twitch is so satisfying, I have no clue, but I don't have time to question such things when the limo stops, and the sound of chatter infiltrates the otherwise quiet car.

"Yes! We're here!" Hans exclaims as he and Celina scoot out, leaving me and Matty inside.

Mateo regards me seriously as he says, "That's it. For the sake of humanity and all that is holy in rock and roll, tonight we're getting you laid."

"Excuse me!" I don't think twice about setting my hand on his, stopping him.

When I realize what I've done, he looks at me, then at my hand as he slowly pulls it away. I watch as he flexes his palm, his weight shifting closer to me, nearly boxing me in.

"I mean, I don't need to, like, hire a person, at a sex club like a... I mean I—" God, I sound like an idiot.

Mateo laughs, and the sound is like smooth, top shelf bourbon.

Not that I'd know what that tastes like, but it's what I imagine.

Everything about this man reeks of *sophistication.*

"Can't write a song about a good fuck if you haven't experienced it," he says, flashing me with a wicked grin.

I don't know why I word vomit the worst fucking response ever. I blame it on the martinis.

"Oh and you have?" I bite.

Matty chuckles darkly. "I'm not legally allowed to tell you," he says smoothly. "Besides, I'm not paying for your lap dances. You're going to have to work for it on your own, kid."

I purse my lips as a fresh flood of irritation spreads like wildfire.

I can pay for my own lap dance, thank you very much, Matty!

"But the clientele here are more than... suitable. For your needs, I think."

His dark gaze catches mine for a moment as he leans in closer to me.

So close, his breath on my neck is warm, and I can smell his cologne. It smells like sex and chocolate, and makes my mouth fucking water.

What does he know about *my* needs?

He doesn't know shit about me.

"A little tip?" he breathes, and my gaze falls to his perfect, pouty lips.

I think all the sugar has rotted my brain. My gaze flashes up to his as I await his words like candy.

"Sure..." I swallow, my mouth going dry.

"If you want someone to want you, Dare, you have to want yourself. Know what you bring to the table, kid. Then make them fucking beg for it."

Stupidly, I whine in defeat. "I have no clue what I bring to the table," I say like an idiot. "Except maybe rice crispy treats. Those are nice..."

Matty smirks. "Then maybe you should find out." He coughs, his voice like an echo in the cavernous space.

And before I can protest, he scoots out of the car, leaving me in the darkness.

And at that moment, I've never wanted to impress anyone the way I want to impress Mateo Starr.

Fake it 'til you make it, right?

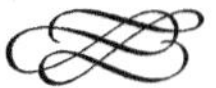

Mateo

"It's so…" Geo swallows, shifting a little closer to me.

"Relaxing?" I taunt as I elbow him, finding a bit of solace in his reaction.

"I was going to say…bright," he snarks, crossing his arms as a waitress in a white and blue angel uniform squeezes past us.

"Oh, that's just Saint's aesthetic. The dungeons are downstairs. Where the real sinners go," I say, unable to hide my laugh. "And the Hell aesthetic is stereotypically black and red."

While Geo may have transitioned from his

Christian rock schtick a while ago, I can't say I've ever seen the man at a strip club, period, let alone one like Saint & Sinner.

But it's somehow so much better than I ever imagined, and I'm never going to let him forget this.

I take a sip of my drink as I sink back into the white leather booth, watching as Hailee and Celina drag Hans and Richie across the floor.

"Dungeons? Like Dungeons and Dragons?" Dare's saccharine voice cuts through like a knife.

I turn to see him wide-eyed as he glances at the crowd, which is pretty heavy for so early in the night.

"You've got to be kidding me," I drawl as Geo attempts to pour himself a glass of champagne the waitress dropped off.

Dare turns to look at me in earnest as if I've interrupted him.

"What are you even still doing here? Aren't you supposed to be out there?" I motion to him to leave.

Geo side-eyes me as he clutches his drink. "What about you? You just going to sit here all night like a Kingpin?" he snips.

I regard him with an annoyed expression. "I do not engage."

"You like to watch, is that it?" Dare raises an eyebrow at me as he goes for a glass of champagne, proceeding to add about six strawberries to the glass. Barely any liquid will fit in there, but I suppose where Dare is concerned, that might not be a bad thing.

After all, I'm not fixing for a replay of Sylvestro's mansion. Perhaps I should keep an eye on him.

Just for safety's sake.

"What I like is none of your fucking business. Besides, you're stalling."

"Stalling for what?" Geo's gaze drifts to another host, a man wearing tight white shorts and a set of fluffy wings.

"Our darling little *Heart Killer* has a mission tonight," I quip with a grin as Dare stops mid pour.

"What's that?" Geo asks, and I can tell he's sweating.

"Find someone to fuck."

Geo nearly spits out his champagne as Dare curses.

I slap Geo on the back as he coughs.

"And what about you, Matty? You take a vow of celibacy I don't know about?" Dare's gaze meets mine as he slurps his champagne.

My palm twitches and my jaw tenses. I'm going to need a lot more than champagne and three Nikka's to get through this night if he keeps his shit up.

"No," I bite.

Geo regains himself as he shifts his stance.

"Maybe *you* should engage for once. Put yourself back out there," Geo says plainly.

I have half a mind to tell him to fuck off, before Dare *grabs* me by the hand and pulls me up.

I stumble, almost knocking him over as Geo grins.

"Maybe that's why *you* have an attitude, Matty. Maybe *you* need to get fucked," Dare taunts me, throwing my words back at me.

He doesn't let go of my wrist, his palm against my skin sweaty and warm.

My heart feels like it may explode from the touch, the warmth.

I feel as if I am on the edge of a dangerous cliff, with Darren Wylde and his stupid golden retriever energy.

And perhaps it's the alcohol I've consumed, or the light that shines from the stage over the crowd, or perhaps it's Geo smacking me on the back.

But I find myself powerless to resist Dare's touch, or his pleading, puppy dog eyes.

Fuck, I'm going to need another drink.

When we reach the floor, I find Hailee and Richie dancing together, alongside Celina and Hans, who have somehow ended up with glitter all over them.

Hailee's gaze catches mine and she smiles.

"Well, well, look who decided to leave the castle," she says with a laugh.

Richie stiffens, moving back enough to give her space, and I don't miss the flash of fear in his eyes.

I scare him, and that should excite me, but instead it only makes me feel like an asshole.

A waitress offers us test tube shots, and I don't think twice about taking one, if only to quell the sudden emotion that has me feeling so... human.

"Oooh, I want one," Dare says as his fingers brush against mine.

I shoot him a glare. "Careful, Dare." I say as I

grip my test tube. "You wouldn't want to *forget* this epic night, would you?"

Dare scoffs as he downs his shot, then *grabs* mine out of my cold hands. He downs it, too.

"Last I checked, you're not the boss of me, Matty." He slams down the shot glasses, raising his arms as he sticks his tongue out, and the crowd around us goes wild.

Dare shakes his head back and forth, his silky locks falling in his face as he yells, "*Heart Killer* and *Mage Of Mercy* are in the fucking house!"

Richie whoops and Celina and Hans scream.

I watch, frozen, as everyone in our proximity falls into his energy, his space.

Including a man who looks to have been glitterbombed, dressed in a white linen shirt, speckled with glitter dust.

He's young, blond, and attractive, and Dare doesn't even see the way he's looking at him.

The way *everyone* looks at him.

Hollywood is full of tanned, toned, and plastic idols, but Dare would stand out of a crowd anywhere.

Some people just have that magnetism, that fabled "it" factor that draws people in like a moth to a flame.

Darren Wylde has that fire, and the throngs of people around us can't help but be drawn to him.

The attractive blond comes up behind him, placing his hand on Dare's waist, whispering in his ear. Dare stiffens, but turns his head, his jet black hair shimmering in the light as he looks at the man with a grin and I feel a stupid sense of pride melding with a foreign emotion I haven't felt in years.

I have no right or reason to be *jealous.*

Dare is not *mine.* Not even anywhere close.

I grab myself another shot and shoot it, needing to numb the pain, the emotion that threatens to take me under. Emotions I thought I had meditated the fuck away.

I scan the crowd, looking for someone to distract me from this moment. This was a bad fucking idea.

As a rule of thumb, I often try to keep my personal life and my dominant life separated for a reason.

The dungeons call to me, my twitching palm.

Down in the Sinner's playground, I can breathe.

Up here, with Hailee, Geo...

With Dare rolling his hips, throwing his head back with a stupid ass grin while he lets strangers *touch* him...

I feel powerless.

"Where are you going, Matty?" Dare asks as I head for the bar.

Champagne isn't going to cut it this time. I need something stronger.

Something that will make me not give a shit.

I don't bother answering him, not until his hand is wrapped around my wrist, warm and moist against my skin. I stop at the steps and turn around, shaking his touch from me, even though I hate it.

I hate that I *like* his warmth.

I hate that just that small fucking touch makes me feel *better*.

"What's wrong? Did I do something wrong?" he asks, those dark pleading puppy dog eyes pulling my heartstrings.

Heart Killer is more than an appropriate name for Dare fucking Wylde. Because damn if am not bleeding from his fucking sweetness, hungry for a fucking bite.

"No," I say as my jaw tenses. "I just need a fucking drink."

Dare furrows his eyebrows. "Then let me buy you a drink, man. It's the least I can do. I mean, you got us in here, got the damn VIP..."

I know I should say no.

I should turn Dare around and push him toward the little twink who would probably give him everything he needs for a good song.

But something about his eyes, his pouty lips, his dark, silky hair falling across his shoulders kills any resistance.

I fight the desire to reach out and run my hands through it.

This is a bad, bad idea.

"Fine." I give in as I try to find my ground. "One drink."

THE LIGHTS ARE blue and white, and everything is a blur.

An endless blur of drinks and bodies, and heat. So much fucking heat.

I slide my fingers over the hands that grip my waist as I close my eyes. I let them guide me, guide us, in rhythm. Usually, I refrain from the dance floor because I've never been much of a club-goer.

But there's something blissfully wonderful about not knowing anyone's name when the lights are burning down on you. At least, for me.

Though their touch isn't warm and it doesn't make my cock twitch, combined with the drinks I've had, it's enough to level me. It's enough to *distract me.* To make me...

Normal, I guess.

I rock back and forth as I open my eyes, watching the stage.

At some point, we all gravitated toward the front for the nightly Angel's performance set.

Dare and Richie are having the time of their lives, dancing, drinking. Even Hailee looks happier than I've ever seen her, but then again, that may have to do with all the free-flowing alcohol on my dime.

A strange sense of pride fills me as I watch my sister, our friends... and even Dare—especially Dare—enjoy themselves.

It feels good to give other people happiness, even though I know I'll never have it myself.

That kind of stuff isn't mean for a fucked up person like me.

Edward proved that.

I stop as I see Dare *climb* on stage, and everyone in the crowd screams.

"What's he doing?" I ask, my words sounding slightly slurred to my own ears.

"Such a noble volunteer!" the redheaded angel says as she motions to Dare.

Dare grins like the Cheshire Cat, and under the bright lights, he looks like he really is having the best night of his damn life.

I rock back and forth with the nameless man whose hands slide up and down my waist, but they are cold and clammy.

I want warmth.

So, I gravitate toward the fire.

I wriggle away from the man holding me and step up toward the edge of the stage. Another angel brings out a chair while an angel with short blonde hair carries a red towel or something in her arms.

"Now, be a good little boy and do as we say and we'll take you to heaven," Angel number one says, and Dare charismatically winks at the crowd before sticking his pink tongue out again. Naturally, the crowd cheers.

I watch as he sits on the steel chair, raising his eyebrows and smiling.

I grip the bar in front of me while my friends and anonymous individuals stuff money in between the bar for the girls.

I watch as the redhead angel opens the buttons of his neon green shirt, slowly, while some techno-beat makes the bass throb all around us. She moves the flaps, exposing his large, tattooed chest, while another angel takes his hands behind the chair, proceeding to tie them with red silk ribbon.

Angel number one runs her hands over his chest—which I note sports a large tattoo over smooth, pale flesh—while angel number two tugs on the silk ribbon that binds his wrists together, noting that they are tight, as angel number three proceeds to work on tying his ankles to the chair, while angel number one plays with his nipples, thrusting her heavy breasts in his face, then pulling back.

Dare's pale chest glistens under the light. His signature tattoo—a heart with black wings framing his pecs—draws contrast to his dark nipples, and I notice the slivers of silver glinting in the light between her fingers.

I'm mesmerized by the sight as I think about his pain tolerance. Nipple piercings fucking hurt. They also look appealing on him, and I can't help but think about what his reaction would be to my steel clamps. The images, thoughts of such things threaten to pull me under.

The red ribbon contrasts his pale skin, and he leans his head back, craning his neck to look up at the angel, lips pouty and eyes full of heat.

My gaze travels down his soft curves, the way the silk ribbon cuts across his flesh, drawing shadows across his hipbones, down to the evident hardness displayed and accentuated by his bondage and tight black jeans. He might not be as cut and hard-edged as most of the men in this industry, but fuck if the sight of him bound doesn't make me want to grab his soft hips, to sink my fingernails into what is probably a perfect, plump ass, to watch it pink from my handprint or the sting of a whip.

To stroke and soothe the pain I cause until my marks disappear.

Angel number one straddles him as angel number two runs her hands along his chest, playing with his nipples.

"Such a good boy you are!" Angel one giggles as she addresses the roaring crowd.

Dare groans, but he doesn't move. He doesn't grind or shift or fight at all.

Realization hits me like the crack of a whip.

He likes this.

The women, the ropes.

The commands.

Being the center of attention.

And like a dying moth, I can't turn away from his fire, even though I know he's going to burn me to fucking pieces.

But that's my problem, isn't it?

For all the control I favor, I am Icarus, and I crave the fucking sun.

My cock throbs as I watch the angels touch him, tease him.

Jealousy pools once again within me like a cyclone, bringing back the memories of my downfall.

I've always known my interests were niche. I like men, and I like men who need to be broken. Because I'm fucking broken.

I can't compete with soft breasts and tight pussy.

And from the sight before me, it's more than clear that Dare *likes* that.

And because I truly am a glutton for punishment, and I am buzzed enough to not give a shit, I close my eyes for a moment, and I let my thoughts wander places they shouldn't.

I imagine the angels around Dare have disappeared, and I am in their place. Tying, twisting, touching him.

Imagining the feel of his soft skin under my palms, his taut, pierced nipples sensitive from the clamps. The stiff texture as I bite and lick them, as he wriggles beneath my touch, his hardness growing against my own.

The groan that would escape his throat as I wind him up like a fucking music box with just my touch.

Listening to his moans because he can't touch himself, bound in my ropes.

Begging me for mercy, to make him come.

Swallowing down every drop of his sweet release and then doing it all over again, edging him, until he begs me to stop, spent from the pleasure.

I swallow harshly as my cock strains against the inside of my pants at the thought of the endless pleasure. I grab myself, if only to stave off the desire, opening my eyes.

Dare's dark gaze stares directly at me, and it is like he truly sees me. Or through me, I'm not entirely sure. Because I feel like a ghost.

Haunted by my own choices, my own vices.

My heart beats so loud I think the whole club can hear it as I get lost in the perfect performance before me.

He's drunk, strung up on display for all of Saint & Sinner to see, and I know better than anyone how a crowd can drown everything out.

How cathartic and blissful it can be under those lights.

How being bound can be so fucking freeing that you forget about everything else.

I've always been dominant, by nature, but that doesn't mean that I have no experience being a submissive. But I haven't trusted anyone enough to play switch in a long fucking time. Not since I was probably Dare's age.

Moisture pebbles my cockhead as I think about how pretty he'd look in my Italian leather ropes.

Naked and exposed, begging for mercy.

A hand settles on my shoulder, jolting me

from my dreams, and I remember where I am and that I am not alone. Not by a long shot.

"I need to go," I mutter as I shove off the touch of a stranger.

I turn around, but I stumble, nearly knocking over a waitress. I apologize, heading for the one place I know I can be free.

A man dressed in a leather harness and leather shorts stops me at the velvet rope.

"Do you have a reservation?" he asks plainly. I shake my head, my cock throbbing, knowing salvation is not far away.

"I'm fucking Mateo Starr. I have a standing reservation."

The man purses his lips as he pulls up his information on his tablet, and I scowl.

In the distance, I can hear someone calling my name.

The devil, himself, perhaps?

My fucking sanity?

"My apologies, Mr. Starr. Room seventeen is open."

He opens the rope and I can barely concentrate on anything.

CHAPTER 9

Everyone thinks that rockstars come out of the mold ready to fuck shit up.

But the truth is, most of us are a lot more nerdy and un-cool in our early years, and most of the badass shit is just an act.

It's a job. At least, that is what I told myself when we signed with Casualty Records.

Whatever they want you to be, be it.

Matty's words echoed in my brain, telling me the only way to attract ass was to want my own.

I'd taken those words to heart, more than I think he meant for me to.

So, I did the only thing I could. I performed.

I channeled the visage of badass mother-fucker, the kind of man who doesn't give two shits about anything except having a good time.

And it worked.

So good, I actually believed it myself.

And for a little while, I felt like the person I always wanted to be.

I drank with my damn idol, danced with hot guys, got tied up by pretty angels...

Life was fucking awesome.

And when I opened my eyes, staring out at the audience, I saw *him.*

Standing at the edge of the stage, eyes closed, *grabbing* himself, and when he opened his eyes, he looked right fucking at me.

Like he knew every thought in my fucking brain.

I couldn't take my eyes off of him, or the way he licked his lips, or the obvious fucking tent in his pants.

Because he was watching me.

Something about that realization seemed important, but at the time, it was white noise.

Because the only functioning brain cell I had

at the moment was screaming that Mateo fucking Starr was *watching me.*

And he liked what he was watching, that was obvious.

But then he ran away.

And I am bound, tied to a fucking chair, and I can't get to him.

My dream turns into a nightmare as panic and heat flush through me.

When the angels finally set me free, I practically jump off the stage, nearly taking out Hans and Celina. I look around us, but I don't see anyone else.

"Where did everyone go?" I ask.

"VIP maybe?" Hans shrugs.

"Maybe they went to get fresh air?" Celina says.

I scan the room, but my sight is blurry to begin with from the bright lights, not to mention the copious amounts of alcohol in my system.

Every time Matty told me to take it easy, I just went harder, because I didn't want to look like a fucking pussy in front of him.

One drink had turned into at least four and I was half certain the man was trying to out drink me or something just to prove a point.

But I am too fucked to care what that point was, because the more I drink, the better I feel, and the more I believe in my performance.

I'm, like, Leo DiCaprio method acting or some shit.

I push my way through the crowd, heading for VIP, but the only person left is Geo, who seems to be much more interested in his phone.

"Where did he go?" I ask.

Geo looks up at me, raising an eyebrow. "Who?"

"Fucking Matty," I huff, only slightly out of breath.

Geo's lips pull at the corners. "Probably heading to the Sinner's Playground." He shrugs. "Especially, after *that* titillating theatrical performance of yours."

I'm too fucking drunk to know what that even remotely means, but Geo takes some pity on me and points me in the right direction. "He's talking to the ringmaster as we speak."

I follow Geo's direction to see Matty's tall frame, his shoulders, waiting at the velvet rope, and I don't think twice. I leap down the steps and I run.

Chasing something I'm not quite sure I understand.

Maybe I have it all wrong. Maybe he's just fucking wasted, too, and forgot where he was.

Maybe it has nothing to do with *me.*

I call his name, but he can't hear me.

Or worse, maybe he does and he's fucking ignoring me. Like the asshole he is.

Except I thought... I thought maybe with all the whiskey and all the dancing... maybe Mateo Star was actually starting to thaw.

Maybe he isn't a cold, bitter asshole.

Because as we all danced under the lights, side by side, I could have sworn he looked like he was having *fun.*

I reach the ropes just as he disappears and the attendant looks at me with disdain.

"I'm with him, obviously," I bite. The devil in leather only raises an eyebrow.

"Do you have a reservation?" he deadpans.

"Do you know who I am?" I bite, frustrated and drunk as shit.

Not that I go around touting my fame like a hall pass, ever.

The man sighs. "Yes, I know who you are, Mr. Wylde."

"Then you better open this fucking rope or I'm going to give this place one hell of a Yelp review."

Honestly, I'm surprised my threat works.

But it does.

The man grumbles about not being paid enough for this shit, and mumbles something about room seventeen.

And then I see him, heading toward the far end of a dark hall, lit up by red neon lights.

"Matty, wait!" I call, huffing as I catch up to him.

He freezes, beneath the shadows of the hallway, just out of reach from the lounge.

I come up against him, noticing several closed doors in the alcove but otherwise it's empty.

"Matty…" I barely get the words out before he grabs me, throwing my back against the wall.

"Why?" he growls, sliding his hand up my arm, across my neck.

His fingers twitch against my throbbing vein there, like he's afraid.

But I'm not sure why anyone in their right mind would be afraid of a two hundred pound man with an open neon shirt, enough rolls to start a bakery, and ripped jeans.

I might look slightly menacing when I'm done up for a press shoot, but otherwise...

"Why, what?" I breathe, my cock twitching from his close proximity, from the heat of his palm against my skin. My skin feels flushed from a mixture of my run and the way he's looking at me.

I look up at his dark eyes, and they remind me of starry skies.

Vast and all encompassing at the same time. The neon red light makes him look every bit like a devil, hungry for my fucking soul.

God, do I want to be devoured.

"Why do you keep calling me that, when I ordered you not to?" he says, through gritted teeth. "Why are you so defiant?" His fingers squeeze my neck, and the touch is surprisingly gentle, given the heat and the tone of his voice.

"Why do you fucking bait me?" he says, his dark gaze falling to *my* lips.

I'm powerless underneath his touch, his gaze.

I can't speak, under his spell.

All I can do is focus on my cock, because

Matty leans against me, and I know he can feel my fucking erection.

Because I can feel *his*.

My heart beats like a drum as I lick my lips.

And because I'm drunk, I don't think twice about saying shit I know I shouldn't.

"I fucking bait you?" I growl, pushing back against his chest. My nipple ring catches on his silk shirt, tugging a bit, but I don't feel pain.

All I feel is *alive*.

"How am I supposed to keep up with your fucking moods? One minute you're a dick, the next you're renting limos because you think it's what I want," I snap.

"I didn't rent the limo for you, little shit."

"Yes, you did." I push my body against him, knocking him back against the wall on the opposite side. His back thuds against the wall, and I don't miss the shock in his gaze.

The way his eyes glisten causes my cock to twitch, igniting a fire within me I know isn't entirely to blame on the alcohol.

I brace my hands on the wall beside his shoulders.

He's got a few inches on me, so I have to look up at him.

His chest rises with heavy breaths.

He grabs my neck, his hand around my throat.

I'm far too keyed up, far too drunk, and far too past the point of fucking caring.

I throw my last operating brain cell to the wind as I crush my mouth against his like an avalanche.

Matty's body stiffens beneath me, but he opens his mouth.

He fucking opens *his mouth.*

He pulls away for a moment, eyes wide with shock.

And then he *pulls* me against him, setting one hand on the exposed flesh of my hip, while the other squeezes my throat and fucking *kisses me back.*

The reality is too much to comprehend.

All I know is that I want more.

I press my body against him, pinning him to the wall. His cock twitches against my own, and clearly, I've lost all my marbles in this fucking place, because the words that come out of my mouth are *not* mine.

They can't be, because I would never say, "You like that, don't you?"

Matty bites my lower lip with his teeth before plunging his tongue into my mouth, which only fuels my temporary bout of insanity.

"Fucking hell, Dare..." Matty's voice is blurry, like my vision.

I thrust my hips against him, rubbing my erection against his, and he curses in my mouth.

"I want you to beg for it," I growl.

"Fuck," Matty groans. "No," he fights. "I will not!"

I thrust myself against him, kissing, licking, and doing everything I can to keep this version of Matty alive. He groans as I do so, so I keep doing it.

Because I can't deny I like him like this.

Hard, needy, and fucking beneath me.

"This is what I bring to the table," I say like a fucking idiot. "And I'm going to make you fucking beg for it." I flash him a lecherous grin.

Somewhere in my drunk mind, I think that's a zinger.

"Fuck!" Matty growls in return, shivering beneath my weight.

He pulls away from me, breathing heavy as he drops his hand between us, cursing again.

"Fuck, fuck, fuck!" he barks out, turning away from me, and I fall back against the wall, losing my footing.

"I can't do this, I can't..." Matty pulls out his phone.

I fall on my ass.

"I'm calling the driver back. I think it is time we ended this nightmare." He punches a number into the lit screen.

Nightmare.

He called me a nightmare.

Fuck.

I fucked up.

Bad.

"Matty, I–"

"Be out front in ten minutes, Dare," he snaps, his voice cold, calculating.

Gone is the needy, sexy Batman that pushed me over the edge, and in its place is the bitter musician who thinks I'm the bane of his damn existence.

My eyes glisten as shame and guilt rack me, because the way he looks at me cuts me to my core.

It's the opposite of praise.

It's remorse.

No, no, no...

He starts to walk away, leaving me in the shadows of this empty hallway.

He is halfway before he turns around.

A deep sigh leaves him as he grabs me, attempting to lift me up.

He wraps my hand around his shoulder and holds my waist, and a sob tears through me as I lean against him.

"Matty, I—"

"Darren, for once, fucking listen to me. Please. Don't." His voice softens for a moment. "You'll forget about it in the morning, anyway."

A part of me recognizes the sadness, the loneliness in his voice. I want to tell him I won't, that I could never forget him and his sexy grin or his Batman voice, or the hunger in his eyes while he watched me on stage.

And I would never forget the way his fingers felt when they squeezed my neck, the way his tongue felt in my mouth, or the truth that lay buried underneath walls of stone.

I could never forget Mateo Starr crumbling underneath me if my life depended on it.

"Where are we going?" I ask like a sad little kid.

"I need to keep you safe." He guides me through the crowd, his grip on my waist solid and firm.

"Are you mad?" My stomach flips, fear shaking my tired bones, and I feel like I might throw up.

Should I tell him that?

"You are asking me if *I* am mad?" He scoffs.

"Yeah, you seem like you're mad..." I mumble as we reach the cold air out outside. I try to stifle my sniffle, but I can't. I feel like the biggest asshole ever. "Like you're mad at me."

Matty guides me into the limousine, and I all but fall over onto the seat. The leather is chill against my skin and makes me feel a fraction better.

Matty sighs, trailing his fingertips down my back, letting his hand settle on the small of my back, which isn't small by any means. He gently rubs my exposed skin, his touch warm and smooth.

I like it too much to pretend I don't.

I'm hot, sweaty, drunk, and feel like shit. Also, I might throw up in this car.

He'll be really mad then.

"No, Dare," he says softly, like a tired Batman. "I'm not mad at you. Go to sleep."

My eyes are heavy, and I don't have the will to fight his order.

CHAPTER 10

DARE

FUCK. I'm hungover. Again.

I grab for my pillow to shield my eyes. It's way too fucking bright in here. I need to seriously tell Penny to knock it off with the curtains.

My fingers slide along something velvet, and immediately, I tense. I don't own fucking velvet *anything*.

I open my eyes, and panic hits me instantly. The room I'm in is enormous, and full of windows. Like, floor to ceiling windows, and all I can see for miles is forest.

I look up, seeing the ceiling is also replaced by windows.

It's like a human terrarium.

Or an observatory.

With a really, really lux bed.

Like, I think you could easily fit five people in this damn thing.

I rub my eyes, trying to remember what happened. One look under the deep blue velvet covers lets me know my get fucked mission was a failure, because I'm still in my fucking underwear.

I fall back against the pillows, looking straight up through the window ceiling at the cloud-filled sky.

I clutch the soft covers to me. They smell masculine and woodsy, and the whole place feels moody, but somehow comforting.

I look to the nightstand, and suddenly I'm tense once more. I see a note card with my name on it, next to a tall glass of water, and a bottle of ibuprofen, set in one of those trays people serve drinks on.

I reach over and gingerly take the note card with my name on it, flipping it open with fear.

I swear if this is my Squid Game letter, I'm fucked.

Inside is the fanciest writing I've ever seen.

Take two ibuprofen and drink the entire glass of water.

Towels and clean clothes are on the counter in the en suite bathroom.

Shower is not negotiable.

Your presence is required in the kitchen immediately following your shower.

It's signed with just an M, and of course, included on the bottom of the card is fucking *directions* to the kitchen.

I twist my lips as heat floods my entire being and my stomach flips, and suddenly, I am assaulted by my blurred memories of the prior night.

Of Matty, loading me into his limo, and telling me we were going somewhere "safe."

No wonder the card of instructions sounds so damn bossy.

I look at the tall glass of water and contemplate not doing what he says.

But my stomach growls, my head aches, and I feel hot and gross.

So I shove down the need to defy this

asshole's orders, take my damn ibuprofen, and find the glass of water tastes really good.

And I'm fucking parched.

I don't get up immediately, though, because this bed is really fucking warm and soft, and I want to commit the feeling to memory.

I'm gonna shoot across the sky like a beam of light

Gonna ricochet off the walls of the night

The words come to me easily, but fuck...

Panic floods me as I realize I don't know where my clothes are, or my phone.

I throw myself out of bed, regrettably. This guest room is huge, but it isn't messy by any means, and I don't see my clothes or my phone *anywhere.*

Shit.

I make my way to the en suite bathroom, and I swear it's bigger than my bedroom.

Decked out in black marble with gold etchings, the floor, wall, and shower all look like something out of one of those old epic movies. Like Cleopatra or some shit.

It's still moody as fuck, but pretty.

Like Matty.

True to the card, there are dark blue towels—

four to be exact—piled atop the black marble counter, next to what looks like a pair of gray sweatpants, a white shirt, and a pair of black boxer briefs. There's even a pair of slides that look like they might actually fit my size thirteen feet.

It's kind of weird, but also kind of comforting, and I hope he didn't go too out of his way to find this stuff.

Who am I kidding, he probably has staff for this sort of thing.

I doubt Matty actually went to the trouble, given the fact he's probably hungover as shit, too.

I don't waste time as I climb into the shower, my headache already starting to ease up.

Guess the ibuprofen wasn't such a bad idea.

Thankfully, the shower doesn't take me too long to figure out, though it's a little space age for my liking. After about five minutes of fumbling with the settings, I get it to a warm temperature, and the steam starts to build. The Eucalyptus hanging around the faucet makes the place smell like a spa, and I can't help but close my eyes and relax for a moment as the hot water sluices over my skin.

There's barely anything stocked in the

shower, and I have no idea what dispenser is shampoo, conditioner, or body wash, so I eeny-meeny-miny-mo it and hope for the best.

Whatever the case, the stuff smells like fucking heaven.

It smells like Matty.

Instantly, my memories burst through at the thought of his name, as everything comes crawling back.

The drinks, the dancing, the angels.

The *kiss.*

I fucking kissed Matty.

My muscles tighten as I curse in the small space.

And he kissed me back. I can't have imagined that.

Or his fucking dick grinding against me.

My cock remembers, too, apparently, because the moment *that* particular memory fills my psyche, the appendage twitches and hardens.

I swallow harshly as I remember his groans, his tongue in my fucking mouth.

The hot water runs down my skin and I close my eyes, letting my forehead fall against the black tile.

I take my cock in my hand, and I let out a deep sigh as I stroke myself.

It's always been part of my morning routine while I shower, and I have a feeling if I don't take care of this right now, it's going to make the morning a lot more awkward than it already is.

Because last night I fucking kissed the man of my teenage dreams, and he opened his fucking mouth.

For me.

With the scent of his shampoo and body wash mixing with the eucalyptus, and the steamy thoughts filling my brain of Matty's tongue against mine, of his fucking hardness against mine, his hands around my throat... it doesn't take me long.

I suck in a breath as I rock my hips, stroking my cock with steady, fast rhythm.

The drag of my cock through my warm, wet fist is a welcome relief, and I come hard and fast with a deep groan and Matty's name escaping my lips in a whispered hiss.

The water sprays around me, washing my guilt and my cum down the drain.

My shoulders sink as I pump some more of what I hope is body wash and not shampoo into my hands, cleansing myself once more to make sure I've washed *all* the evidence away.

When I'm done, I flip off the water, get out, and towel off, noting the towels themselves are softer than anything I've ever felt.

A part of me wishes I could stay here. In this nest of soft beds and towels, surrounded by the forest.

It's a sort of comfort and peace I never knew existed, but now that I do...

I'm more than surprised the boxer briefs fit perfectly. I've never been much of a briefs guy in general, mostly because I like things a bit looser, but I can't deny that when I put them on, they make my junk look huge, and that itself makes me feel pretty good.

I grab the note card, if only to follow the directions to the kitchen, and surprisingly, it's a lot easier than I thought. I marvel at the black walls and exquisite paintings and photographs lining the walls as I make my way down the hallways to the kitchen.

I have to remember to breathe, because as I come up to the crisp, white room, Matty looks like a fucking *god*.

His slender, black-fitted frame stands out against all the white. He's fully dressed in his usual gothic-looking attire; a black shirt with the sleeves rolled up to showcase his badass constellation tattoos, black pants, and shoes.

He's always dressed like he's going to a fucking funeral, and I've always kind of dug that about him.

"Sit." He says the words solidly, like a command.

Part of me wants to argue with him on principle, but another part of me... the part that is connected to my fucking cock, kind of likes when he's being bossy Batman.

God, what is wrong with me?

I don't make any comment, though, and instead, do as he demands.

I take the seat next to him, swiveling on the bar stool, and he gets up immediately, leaving me alone.

I frown as I realize he's probably pissed at me because of what happened last night.

God, I'm such an idiot.

I watch as he opens his refrigerator, and pulls out a bowl and a tall glass of green liquid.

He slides both in front of me, grabbing a spoon and setting it beside the bowl as he watches me intently. He doesn't sit down, though, nor does he say anything. I peek at the bowl, which looks like cold oatmeal, and I sniff the glass of green gunk. It smells good, like pineapple, but it looks gross as hell.

"Is breakfast negotiable?" I ask casually.

"No." Matty says matter of factly, turning away from me to head toward what looks like a Keurig on steroids.

"How do you know I'm not allergic to any of this shit?" I bite, crossing my arms.

"I spoke with your manager this morning."

My eyes widen. "What?" I nearly choke on my cold oatmeal. "Shit! I totally forgot, Penny—"

"Well, I had to inform her of your... late arrival," he says, crossing his arms. "Besides, I take the health of my... guests seriously."

Oh. Right.

Stupid Dare! Of course...

I poke at the oatmeal sludge with a spoon. It jiggles and I'm certain it's not supposed to do that.

"When you are finished, we will head to the studio."

I look back and forth, as if he could be talking to someone else, but it feels like we are the only two people here.

"What? Like... together?"

Matty's jaw tenses.

"Unless you're hiding a micro-machine in your brand new sweatpants, Dare, yes. We are both going to the same place, are we not?"

I take another bite of the cold oatmeal, and it isn't that bad. It's strangely tasty, actually, once you get over the texture thing.

"I guess that makes sense."

"Good." He nods as he pours himself a cup of coffee, watching me intently.

"Do I have something on my face?" I ask, feeling strangely on the spot.

"Did you drink the water?" he asks, deadpan.

I half-contemplate telling him *no*, just to see his eye twitch, but the weird tension in the air tells me that honesty is probably a good policy right now.

"Yes," I say as I finish my bowl of oatmeal.

Matty nods again, sipping his coffee. "Hydration is key for surviving a hangover."

"Thanks," I say as he brushes me off.

"No matter. The car will be here in five minutes."

I slide off my seat, carefully approaching him.

"My phone? Do you, uh... know where it is? Or where my clothes are? I mean, these are nice, but, uh—"

"You don't like them?" he asks, and I almost swear I see a look of disappointment.

"No, I like them. I just..."

Matty slides his hands into his pocket, procuring my phone.

"Keep them," he says cooly.

"Thanks," I say, blinking, my heart pounding in my chest.

"Of course." He hands me my phone, and for a moment, I look at it like it is so much more than a phone.

It feels like it is, anyway.

My fingers brush against his as I take it, and I remember how they felt against my skin. Gripping my throat, stroking my back. My pesky cock remembers, too, stiffening from the memory, and I have to shift my position not to draw attention. With these briefs and sweatpants, it would be far too noticeable.

He pulls away, nodding. "I will have your things delivered to your residence," he says coldly as he heads toward the door.

He turns, his voice softening just a hair. "The car is here."

MATEO

I LET OUT a breath as I pinch my nose, trying to focus on mindfulness, and not on Dare, who is curled up against the side of the window, with his legs curled beneath him.

Memories flash through my brain from the previous night.

The drinks, the angels.

Dare pressing his body against mine, taunting me.

Telling me he was going to make me fucking *beg*.

Something flipped inside me when he made

that comment—threat?—, his words activating something dormant and desperate, and I was so close to giving in. So close to coming, it should be embarrassing.

And knowing that Dare Wylde was somehow capable of infiltrating those abandoned parts of me was terrifying and blissful.

But he was also drunk, and I wasn't in my right mind, either.

Clearly.

And then, I nearly came in my fucking pants like a damn teenager, despite all my tantric training, and that was enough of a sobering moment.

I'm not one for public displays of sex in general, and though the dungeons are private, we were still quite in the open where *anyone* could have seen us.

I'd forgotten where we were.

Because all I could focus on was *Dare.*

On the dark, cocky sound of his voice.

On his sizable hardness twitching against my own.

On the weight of his body pressed against me, like a weighted blanket that smelled like cheap cologne.

On the taste of sour apple martini permeating my tongue.

And I loved every second of it, because, for a single moment, I was free.

I wasn't some heartbroken control freak with a laundry list of kinks.

I was under his fucking spell.

Then, I'd ruined everything with the truth.

Dare would never kiss me if he wasn't drunk.

Because drunk Dare makes bad decisions. Because he's *young*.

Young and stupid.

And I'm a reclusive man on the edge of forty with trust and control issues.

I'm a bad decision, a story Richie and Dare will tell ages from now to a table full of people who will giggle and say, "Oh, those were the days."

But despite all of that, despite my own inebriation, I couldn't find it in me to let the man rot as I had threatened earlier in the day, when he fell on his ass.

Instead, I'd brought him home, undressed him, and taken *care* of him. Because I wanted him to feel better. I wanted to soothe the tears he tried to hide, the loathing that tormented him. I despised seeing Dare so... so...

Unhappy.

Because of me.

And because I wasn't in my right mind, I thought the best place for him to find the comfort he needed, was in my fucking bed. That I could somehow make him understand he's not the problem.

I'm the fucking problem. I'm fucking damaged.

I'm not good for anyone. Hell, I can barely handle my own shit.

I stupidly thought I'd be able to keep my distance if I just slept on the opposite side of the bed. Though, to be fair, my bed is big enough for more than one person. At least I'd know if he was all right, because I would be close. If I would have had my wits about me, I would have slipped him into the guest room down the hall, *far* away from me, where I wouldn't be fucking tempted.

But I woke up at the ass crack of dawn with one arm casually draped across his hip and a solid cock, his back pressed against me, and the chaos inside of me threatened to pull me under.

I shoved him away like he was made of fire, like he'd truly burned me.

Dare only grunted something incoherent in his sleep, and my heart felt like it was going to leap out of my chest.

And the worst part was I felt empty the moment I pushed him away.

Like the burn had scarred me deep below the surface.

That can't happen again. It just can't.

So, I'd done the only thing I could do. As my emotions begged to pull me under, as my breath caught in my throat and panic formed... I focused on what I could control.

I charged his phone, got him some clean clothes. Got a tray of purified water and medicine, fixed a card with instructions, I fed him a suitable breakfast that will keep him energized and feeling better than a greasy breakfast and coffee ever would, and I'd arranged for his things to be returned for him at leisure.

But I still couldn't get the sight of his dark gaze, his perfect lips, or the warmth of his skin against mine, out of my mind.

Nothing, it seemed, would erase Dare Wylde

and his heart killer ways from my psyche. Nothing but distance, of course.

I know that is what I need to do. Rip this splinter out of my fucking skin, tear off this bandaid.

Put some distance between us, so I can *focus.*

Because with Dare around, my attention span seems to falter.

Probably a side effect of spending so much time with someone whose brain is like a squirrel on cocaine.

Dare turns toward me, capturing my gaze.

I've been caught staring. Again.

Fucking hell.

Thankfully, before either of us can say anything, the car rolls to a stop and my driver opens his door.

I breathe a sigh of relief that we are at the studio, and soon enough, I will be able to work out this... this... unsettling energy. Soon, I will lose myself in my music, and everything will be okay.

Dare follows behind me as I swipe my card to let us into the building, and I can feel his gaze on me, like a fire.

I hold the door open for him, nodding for him to enter.

Dare stands there, on the sidewalk, chewing his lip like a piece of licorice.

The sight ignites memory once more, as I recall how soft and plush they were as I nipped at the flesh with my teeth. How they crushed mine with brutal force.

I force the image away as I nod toward the open door and say, "After you."

Dare's eyebrows furrow slightly and he brushes past me, his form sliding against my front only slightly.

I can't deny that he looks good in the basics. Sure, bright colors and dramatic clothing are what he is known for, but there is something about the simplicity of a man in a white tee shirt and gray sweatpants that feels so much... sexier than the former. More intimate.

The shirt itself draws attention to Dare's thick arms, and the array of colorful tattoos that accentuate his skin. It's also tight across his chest, and his nipples prominently poke through, which makes me think of his damn nipple rings, which makes my cock twitch, and...

Lord have mercy on my fucking soul.

"Thanks," he says dejectedly as he enters the building.

With his back to me, I do my best to adjust my cock and close the door.

"Welcome," I say coldly, fighting the urge to say anything else.

The clock reads eleven-thirty, and I sigh. I hate being off on my schedule.

Rehearsals are usually done by three, and usually, I like to head home for a meditation following a rehearsal. Why I let my sister and Geo talk me into going out last night is beyond me.

Clearly, I'm off my game.

Guess I'm going to have to pull some extra hours in the studio tonight to make up for it.

"Matty, listen, I—"

I close my eyes as I give Dare my back. The desire to turn around is strong, but I need to be stronger. I cannot let myself see the remorse, the embarrassment on his face, and know I'm the cause.

I should have put up a fight. I should've said no to that drink, I should've left him in the hallway.

Because if I would have done so, I wouldn't

be standing inches away from him, feeling like the biggest fucking asshole.

"Remember to shut the door," I murmur as I force myself toward my studio room and shut the door tightly.

On the other side of the door, Helena and Palo stand around chatting quietly. One look to the studio and I see it's empty.

"Where's Hailee?" I snap, feeling agitated.

Howler shrugs. "You weren't the only one who called in late this morning," she says. "Hailee said she'd be getting in around noon, probably."

Palo messes with his controls as Helena raises an eyebrow.

"Have fun last night?" she asks, flashing me with a smirk.

"I don't know what you're talking about." I brush past her toward the door to the rehearsal studio.

She doesn't relent, and I sigh in exasperation.

"Oh, come on! Throw me a fucking bone, Mateo!" she whines.

"No," I deadpan, and I throw my guitar strap over my shoulder.

Helena only rolls her eyes. "You're no fun," she chides.

Her words shouldn't bother me, but they do.

Is that really how everyone sees me?

Like some anti-social, mean dick?

I mean, they wouldn't be wrong, but..

I wish not everyone saw me like that.

Just as I've finished tuning my guitar, Hailee walks in.

She's still wearing the clothes she wore last night, her makeup is smudged to hell and back, and overall, she looks like I feel.

Like shit.

I know I *should* say something. Tell her to make better choices. But I know it won't get me anywhere.

It'll only end in an argument, and I'm too fucking tired to fight today.

"Start with *Satellites*?" I ask.

Hailee nods as she turns on her keyboard.

CHAPTER 12

DARE

I MAKE sure the door is shut this time, but I can't deny that there is a part of me that *wants* to defy Matty's orders, just so maybe...

Maybe he'll come tramping down the hallway again and burst through this door, and...

And what, Dare?

This isn't some Disney Channel Original Movie.

This is *life,* and it just isn't fucking fair.

It's like every time I get in the asshole's proximity, I lose my fucking marbles, like the goblins in my brain go out to lunch or some shit.

"Rough night?" Spike drawls, crossing his arms. Like Richie, he's tall, blond, and perfect, down to the chiseled abs and tattoos.

Ines chuckles. "He ain't the only one."

At that moment, my brother walks through the door, looking every bit like a rockstar on a bender.

His blond hair is a mess, sticking out in tufts, and the stain of lipstick on his white shirt isn't hard to miss.

He's also still wearing the same thing he wore yesterday, and Spike whistles.

"Walk of shame, ladies and gents," Ines chirps with a laugh.

Richie's gaze flashes to mine, and I don't think twice about what I say next.

"Oh, and like you assholes have never stumbled in here still drunk from the night before?" I catch my brother's gaze.

"Looks like I'm not the only one who slept in this morning," he says with a grin. He nudges me with his elbow. "Looks like wherever you ended up wasn't so bad."

I roll my eyes as Ines barks in the background.

"I might've scored the comfiest pair of sweats on the planet, but that's it," I grumble with a sigh.

Richie rolls his eyes.

No way in hell am I telling him I woke up in Mateo Starr's house to a bossy musician feeding me Goldilocks porridge.

Some things just don't need to be shared. Especially if you want to preserve those memories.

And lord knows, I'll be preserving the memory of sexy Batman with his hot star tattoos, drinking a coffee in his kitchen in my brain forever.

"Whatever, can we just not do this? I'm tired, my head is killing me, and I just want to get through this damn rehearsal." Richie groans.

Ines and Spike sigh, clearly perturbed that they can't push our buttons anymore.

I swear, if I hadn't of known the guys throughout high school, I'd probably be a lot more pissed off at their shenanigans.

I make my way to stand beside my brother, grabbing my guitar.

He catches my gaze once more.

"Please tell me you didn't wake up with your pants on," I chide.

Richie lets out a tired laugh.

"I woke up handcuffed to my bed. Naked, and hungover as shit."

It was my turn to roll my eyes.

"That why you're late? Elvira Mistress of the Dark leave with the key?"

Richie slides his strap over his shoulder. "Shut up," he says with a laugh, and I can't help but smile.

And for the moment, I feel like that's enough.

BY THE TIME afternoon break rolls around, we're all practically dying for some caffeine. While I would be happy enough with my coffee-not-coffee caramel cappuccino from the break room, Richie is dying for a damn venti with like three shots of espresso, and Penny and the others are more than happy to chime in.

Which is why *Richie* should be the one to be picking up this damn order, but I lost in rock, paper, scissors. Like always.

Though I guess, the walk isn't bad for me, if only because for the first time all day, I feel like I can actually relax.

I slide my hands into my sweatpants pockets, thinking about the last twenty-four hours. Well, the last couple of days, really.

This tour, this whole rockstar thing... it's fucking messing with my head.

On the plus side, outside of my *Heart Killer* costumes and makeup, I mostly look like a washed up Umbrella Academy student with a cake addiction, so thankfully, no one really *notices* me. Especially, with the long hair and sweatpants.

When I enter the Starbucks, I make my way toward the counter to place my order, since the stupid app wasn't working at the damn studio. The line isn't too terrible, about three or four people in front of me, but when I hear a familiar voice cursing *behind* me, I can't help but almost jump out of my skin.

I turn around to see Matty standing there, jaw tight, eyes ablaze.

"Should I get a restraining on your ass?" I tease, feeling a familiar blaze of fire key up in my stomach, in my fucking balls.

Matty's eyebrow twitches and I feel a sense of accomplishment.

And maybe a little better in general.

"Last I checked, it's you who cannot seem to stay away from me," he purrs, his silky voice making my brain turn to mush again.

"Yet here we are." I flash him a smirk and he rolls his eyes.

"The world does not revolve around you, Dare," he grumbles. "My sister, it seems, is in need of caffeine."

I move up, and he does, too. Two people to go.

"And what about you, old man? What do you require? The blood of your haters?"

I watch as his shoulders tighten, and I notice he holds himself rather stiffly.

He's uncomfortable.

Of course, probably because he remembers you making an ass of yourself.

"Nothing that Starbucks can deliver, that's for sure," he mutters on a growl.

Something about his words feel important, and though they sound harsh, I have a feeling it's just his bite.

Beneath it, lies something else, something I can't quite place.

"Richie's dying for some extra kick, too. Then Ines and Spike were like, oh wait, don't forget about me, and then Penny was like—"

I realize I am rambling, so I stop, trying to collect myself and to look like a normal person for once. One person left.

We move up again in the line.

"Can I... can I buy you a drink?" I ask cautiously. I don't miss the way his eyebrows knit together as he contemplates my offer.

"Yes, because that worked so well the last time," he nips.

I know his words should offend me, but they don't.

Not in the slightest. In fact, it's the opposite. They are like a challenge.

"Well, I don't think Starbucks has any whiskey to spike your drink, so I think you're safe." I flash him with a grin.

Matty's eyebrow twitches as he grinds his jaw.

"It's the least I can do, man. You..." I swallow harshly as the words fall out of my mouth without warning. "You took care of my stupid ass, and you didn't have to," I declare, stealing a glance at his steely gray eyes. "More than once."

Matty huffs out a breath. "It is becoming quite a bad habit, I agree," he murmurs, as he nods. "You're up."

I pause for a moment, glancing between him and the barista, and settle on putting my order in. "All right, I need a venti mocha with two shots of espresso," I state as the barista raises an eyebrow.

"Venti already has two shots of espresso, sir. You want four?"

I huff out a sigh of annoyance. "Yes, my brother's like the Walking Dead today. He needs a shock to the heart," I tell her, and she looks at me like I've lost my mind.

Okay, fair.

"Then I need a grande flat white hot, a grande matcha latte hot, and I will have a java chip cookie crumble frappucino, please."

The barista punches her keys, inputting our order, and then I turn to Mateo.

"What do you and Hailee want?"

Matty purses his lips, but I stop him with a finger to his lips so he cannot protest.

"I'm not taking no for an answer. Just tell the pretty lady what you want."

I can swear for the hint of a second, that I feel his tongue against the pad of my fingertips and I drop my hand. The sensation sends a shiver through my body, but Matty looks as stoic and hot as ever.

He narrows his gaze at me. "Fine. If you insist on being a stubborn ass, I will take a venti caramel macchiato with an extra shot of espresso, hot, and I will have an oatmilk chai latte with brown sugar syrup, hot," he demands, adding a sarcastic and dry, "Please."

The way he says *please* makes my damn cock twitch and I have to shift my stance. Again.

I turn away from him, sliding out my wallet to pay for the drinks, but I can feel his gaze on my back like a warm fire.

"Thanks," I say to the barista as I tuck a twenty in the cup for the tips.

Matty and I move down to the opposite end of the counter as the baristas make our drinks.

"You are quite demanding, you know that, right?" he says in his sexy Batman voice.

I can't help but smirk, feeling like I just won the fucking lottery.

"Who me? No. Not at all," I chirp with a laugh. "Not a demanding bone in my body."

"Mhmm," he says as he crosses his arms, bumping into me slightly.

The place isn't all that packed, and I know I can move to give us space, but a part of me doesn't want to.

I don't want to give him the satisfaction, and a part of me likes him being close. Like this.

I can almost pretend he doesn't hate me entirely.

"Darren!" the barista hollers as she slides up the first two drinks.

Matty moves with me, passing me cardboard holders and lids as I set the first two drinks in the carrier.

When the next two drinks come up, he does the same.

"Thanks," I say, flashing him a smile. I notice he glances at me, but his gaze doesn't linger. Not like it did this morning.

But I wish it did.

"I believe it's me who should be thanking you," he replies as the last two drinks are delivered.

I take the last lid from his hands, twisting my lips.

"You're welcome," I say softly as I put the lid on the last cup.

I grab the carrier and Matty walks ahead, opening the door for me.

"Thanks," I say as I squeeze through, brushing against his chest once more. The sun is bright even for the afternoon, and I walk briskly toward the studio. Thankfully, it's only one block away, so it isn't too hot, but a part of me wishes it was further away, if only because I know once we arrive, Matty will disappear again.

And stupidly, I want to keep him here, with me.

I'm such a fucking glutton for punishment.

The air is thick with tension, and I decide I can't take the silence anymore.

"I, uh... had a really great time last night," I say like an idiot. Even to my own ears, I sound lame as hell.

Matty twists his lips, breathing out a sigh. "Yes, well, that makes one of us," he grumbles, and my eyebrows furrow. "I mean... I'm glad. That you... enjoyed yourself," he says cautiously as we come up to the studio street.

I can see the building, and I start to slow down. To my surprise, Matty follows my lead.

"Matty, I—"

I stop on the sidewalk, and he does, too. He looks at me, then at the building, then lets out a sigh.

"You don't have to do this," he says gruffly.

"Do what?" I ask, responding to the tone of his voice. It reminds me of a tiger in a cage. Pacing and pacing, looking regal as shit, but the moment you tap the glass, they show their teeth.

Captive and angry.

"I'm going to make this simple, Darren." His voice trembles as he says my name. He reaches for his drink, and then his sister's.

"Okay..." I say like a confused idiot.

"What happened last night..." He closes his eyes, swallowing harshly. When he opens them again, I can see the sadness, the guilt in his eyes and I fucking hate it.

Because I realize he feels *guilty* about what happened between us.

But why?

Doesn't he know how fucking *hot* he is?

How he drives me fucking crazy?

How I can't stop thinking about him or that fucking kiss?

Or his dick...

"What happened between us last night was a mistake. We were drunk. It can't happen again, and it won't happen again. Do you understand?" He says the words coldly, like he is detached from them.

I've never been considered smart by any means, and I hate being told I can't have something.

It only makes me want it more.

But the desire to fight dies as I see the pain in his gaze.

The loneliness.

The guilt.

And I realize Matty is a caged tiger. He's been in captivity too long. He's afraid of what is beyond his cage.

He's afraid of *me*.

"I understand," I say softly.

And in an instant, those glistening gray eyes shift to something more familiar.

Cold, sexy, and in charge.

"Good. I'm glad we've come to an understanding." He opens the door for me, nodding for me to go in first.

I nod back, feeling a sense of defiance.

I slide through the door, brushing against his body—much more purposefully this time—which places my ass right over his groin.

I don't miss the thinly veiled grunt that leaves his throat, or the way he grinds his jaw.

I smirk even though he can't see me. "Thanks, Matty," I say with sarcasm as I leave him alone once more.

MATEO

WALKING through my house always feels empty, but at least a perk of living with my sister has been that there is always someone here. Well, most of the time, anyway.

But even with a quiet house, I can't concentrate enough to meditate properly.

"You can do this," I say aloud as I crack my neck, straightening my spine. I close my eyes, trying to find my center, but it's no use. My stomach growls, and I sigh in exasperation.

"Guess my chi will have to wait," I mumble to the air as I get up from my mat, slip on my shoes, and head downstairs. Though, even upon opening my fridge, I have no desire to cook anything.

I know I could easily hire a chef like Hailee, but I actually enjoy cooking and baking. There's a sort of comfort in taking all the pieces, all the ingredients, and following the directions that gets me out of my head, even if it's only for a little bit. Plus, I do my best song writing in my brain while I'm cooking.

I suppose I'm irritated because my entire day has been nothing but chaos.

This morning, with Dare... this afternoon... again, with Dare.

And not to mention, my sister was acting weird as fuck all day, and I didn't get as much studio time as I like, not to mention I slept like shit last night.

I take a glance out the kitchen window at the setting sun, making a decision. Stop and grab something comforting from *Mila* for dinner, and head to the studio to get some music therapy. That's just what I need to get my head right.

I don't even bother calling my driver, and decide, for once, to take out my "Fancy Car" as Hailee calls it.

Though I don't think a jet black 1957 corvette is all that fancy, but I digress.

The cool LA air against my skin is refreshing as I drive down the winding road that leads from my house to the studio. I turn on the radio, channel surfing until I land on a station that is more ambient than anything, but I figure that's just fine. The less distractions, the better.

When I finally pull up to the studio with my dinner, it's nearing nine and there isn't a car in sight.

That's one of the things I love about going into the studio late. When it's just me, my guitar, and my thoughts.

Thankfully, the big wigs and the employees at the studio are accommodating and don't bitch too much about my after hours visits. As long as I am making them money, anyway.

I swipe my card and enter the studio, the low lights casting an almost seductive glow on the hallway. I take the elevator up, and as soon as I open the door, I can hear music.

A guitar, acoustic.

No one else is supposed to be here...

I can't help but investigate.

When I finally come to the center of the sound, I sigh in defeat.

He doesn't even see me. He's got his headphones on as he strums away, stopping every couple of seconds to write on a sheet of paper.

He's surrounded by crumpled up paper and a box of half-eaten pizza, still wearing the clothes I gave him.

His dark hair falls in his eyes as he hums out a melody, completely oblivious to anything.

And for a moment, all I can do is watch him process his music, watch as he works.

And then he looks up, and I'm caught once again.

Fuck.

Dare removes his headphones. "I didn't think anyone else was still here," he says quickly.

"They're not. I just got here," I reply carefully.

"What are you doing here?" His eyebrows furrow with confusion as his gaze settles on my brown paper bag full of dinner.

"Sometimes I like to work late," I state firmly.

When I can't focus at home.

"Oh," he says as he absentmindedly strums his guitar.

I should leave. I should turn my ass around and head down the hall, to my studio, and forget about Dare and his puppy dog eyes.

But I find myself unable to resist Dare Wylde, yet again.

"Working on writing your next big hit?" I ask smoothly.

Dare grins, and it's somehow both cheesy and endearing.

"Trying to. I know what I want to write, but it's like my brain goblins have taken a siesta."

I raise an eyebrow. "Your what?"

Dare blushes, shaking his head. "Uh... nothing."

"God, you are certifiable, Dare."

I don't miss the way his eyes light up.

"I think that's a compliment," he says proudly.

And for a moment, I feel relaxed.

Until my damn stomach growls.

"I, uh... guess I'll leave you to it, then," I say as I push off the doorframe.

"Wait..." Dare says, his voice soft.

I hate that I stop dead in my tracks. That just one word can *command* my attention like that.

That *he* can command my attention.

I turn around to look at him. "What?"

"Maybe you could... um..." I watch as his eyebrows knit together, as he struggles with his words.

"English, Dare," I remind him, imploring his gaze with mine. "Take a breath. Use your words."

Dare looks me straight in my eyes, his perfect, pouty lips parted just slightly as he licks his lips with his tongue.

"Maybe you could help me? I mean, sometimes it helps when I play what I have for someone else to hear. Usually, it's Richie, but he's out with the guys, so..."

"You didn't want to go out with your band?" I ask as I enter the doorway, setting my bag down on a table.

I brush off the torn up pieces of paper, sitting on the couch in the corner.

Dare shrugs. "Kinda don't want to end up with a hangover for the third day in a row, you know." He flashes me with a sheepish grin.

I sigh as I open my bag, pulling out the containers containing my meal, a bowl of Korean pork bibimbap and a side order of dumplings with chili crisp.

"Ah, so you can make good decisions," I say, noting the shift in my tone. I hadn't meant to sound so... taunting.

Dare lets out a chuckle as he leans back on his palms, his guitar in his lap. He eyeballs my food with interest.

"What is that?" he asks.

"Spicy as hell," I reply with a shrug of my own. "You probably wouldn't like it."

"I like spicy," he says, sniffing the air, licking his luscious lips. The sight makes my heart beat a little faster and I clear my throat.

"You have your pizza," I nip as I protect my food.

Dare frowns, animatedly.

Like a sad puppy begging for a bite.

Something about the playfulness of his antics, the light in his voice, cuts me deep. I sigh in defeat once more as I hand him the container of dumplings.

"You may have one," I say with sternness

Dare grins as he grabs the container from me. His smile is wicked as he makes direct eye contact while plucking *one* dumpling from the container.

Little brat.

"What seems to be the problem?" I ask.

He devours his prize nearly instantly and hands me back my container, his sticky fingers brushing the edge of mine.

I watch as he licks them clean and proceeds to chew on his fingernails.

"I'm stuck on the chorus," he says, and I toss him a pile of napkins.

"Thanks," he says with a sheepish grin.

When he's done, he strums some chords.

"It's the hook, it just isn't gelling, but I'm not sure what—"

"Play," I command.

To my surprise, he doesn't fight me, just does as I say.

He *obeys.*

"Okay, so... this is what I got..."

The sounds of his acoustic guitar fill the room again as he sings.

"I'm gonna shoot across the sky like a beam of light
Gonna ricochet off the walls of the night
I can't subdue this beating, beating heart
Because I'm not meant to be tamed, honey
I'm meant to be wild, I'm a... a wild star."

Against the acoustics, his voice is beautiful, and I am drawn in once again to Dare's magnetism like he truly is a celestial anomaly.

A bright, shimmering ball of light that can be seen for miles in the darkness.

The way his fingers dance with the chords and frets, the way his shoulders scrunch, the way his dark hair contrasts with his pale complexion.

The emotion behind his voice as he sings.

He's going to blow up one day, I just know it. *Heart Killer* is only his beginning.

"Good start," I say, and it's true. The first verse in its completion sounds pretty good.

"Really?" he asks, his eyes widening.

I twirl some noodles and pork in my chopsticks, nodding. "Yeah," I say, and I slurp them down.

Dare whistles. "Wow, I thought for sure you were going to tell me that it's utter trash," he says as he gestures to his sea of papers.

"Are you the one who writes all your songs?" I ask, genuinely curious.

Dare nods. "Yeah. That's kinda my thing. The band was my creation, which is why Richie said *I* needed to front it. I mean, I love performing, but—"

"You like writing," I say, understanding falling between us.

"Yeah. I do." Dare nods. "Oh! Shit, I'm sorry, you said you needed to rehearse too, right?" He scrambles up off the floor.

I notice he's barefoot, and I can see a small tattoo peeking out from beneath the edge of the sweatpants, on his ankle, across his foot. It looks like... tentacles?

Just how many tattoos has he acquired?

I clear my throat. "Yes, I do, actually. I—"

Dare grabs an electric guitar from the corner. It's neon green with a pink stitched up heart airbrushed on it.

He offers his guitar to me.

"We can take turns," he says, flashing me with a smile that could melt ice.

I look at the guitar, at his fingers curled around the neck.

Somehow, it feels like he's offering me more than just a guitar.

I swallow harshly, my insides swirling again like a cyclone, all the alarm bells in my head starting to sound.

Danger, Mateo! Danger! The sun is too close!

I don't usually play with anyone but Hailee.

But I've always wondered what it would be like to collaborate, to let someone else into my world of music.

Perhaps, I accept his offer because I am curious; perhaps, it is because I am a glutton for punishment.

Perhaps, it is because I don't want to lose the feeling I have right now, where I feel... content and not alone.

I set my chopsticks and my bowl down on the table in front of me and take the guitar from him.

"I don't have anything new I'm working on, unfortunately. Just the same old shit." I strum out the first few notes of Satellites.

"Don't you know your songs by heart at this point?" he asks as he sits down next to me.

I shrug. "Of course I do. But I haven't performed in a while. I want to make sure that this performance, this tour... I need it to be perfect." I say the words with unwavering clarity because it's true. It's what my fans deserve, but also I just want to feel like I am powerful again.

Like I know who I am and what I am good at.

Like I am not astral debris.

Because for the last year, I have felt like a damn fool, and that I've fallen too far from where I once existed.

Stepping away from music for so long... I missed it.

I didn't realize how much I missed it until this moment, as I expertly tickle the chords of Satellites, humming along to the melody.

It's part muscle memory, sure. But for me, it's more than that.

Music is my language. I can express how I feel without having to put it into words.

Words are Hailee's talent, mostly. I learned after we released our third album, *Control*, that even though I loved writing, my tastes were not as commercially palatable. Hailee writes *good* hits. She's been writing for top acts for the last five years while I've been on hiatus, though she rarely gets any actual credit, but she tells me she prefers it that way.

I segway from Satellites into one of my favorite songs absentmindedly.

Control.

I whisper-sing the words, as my fingers remember just how to dance along the frets.

"Here I sit in supplication, careening for your touch

Begging for your forgiveness would never be enough

Strike me, guide me, cleanse my fucking soul

Quiet the chaos baby, give me control"

Dare twists his lips, and a sense of relief floods me as I let the words come easy, getting lost in them once again.

"I don't think you could fuck it up if you tried, Matty," he says, his voice soft and kind.

It's the most genuine I've heard him.

Something about the tone of his voice makes me feel warm, flushed. I fight to look at him as I go into the bridge.

I haven't played this song in ages. Mostly because the label has tried hard to erase the failure of the *Control* album.

"I mean, your playing has always been second to none, and personally, I think you're better than Felix." He flashes me with a smirk. "And your voice is way better. Gravellier." He coughs. "Sexier."

I can't fight the blush that threatens its way onto my cheeks.

I turn away, clearing my throat as I continue

to play *Control*'s melody. It sounds so much different on an acoustic. Softer, but darker somehow.

"Thanks," I reply, but the word is uncomfortable on my tongue.

I'm more than aware of my voice, especially when I perform, both on the stage and behind locked doors.

I learned early on in my career that a voice carries. So, I worked very hard to make mine the kind of voice people would listen to.

But as I sit here, strumming away on Dare's guitar, a part of me recognizes that I am not the same person anymore.

I lost my voice, or perhaps, I left it in the valley with Edward and my broken heart.

And I've been struggling to find it ever since.

Dare leans forward, bracing his tattooed arms on his knees. The couch creaks as I continue to play.

"Your *Control* album got me through some rough days, you know. It's actually what made me want to pursue music more."

I stop at his words, turning to look at him.

He glances at me, and I am stunned.

"You're kidding. No one likes that album. The record execs *hated* it."

Dare shakes his head. "That's cause it's fucking fire. Yeah, it's different from your other stuff, sure. But musicians are meant to explore sound, right? We're supposed to evolve?"

I swallow his compliment along with the sweet, innocent look in his gaze.

"You... know my music?" I don't know why I am so stunned, but something about Dare's admission makes me feel naked and vulnerable. Like with one blow, I could crumble to pieces.

"I mean, yeah. *Mage Of Mercy* was my favorite band in high school." His cheeks flush once more. "You're... kinda the reason I wanted to make music. You and Hailee... you never sounded like anyone else. You were always evolving, changing. Trying new things."

"Yeah. Evolution is inevitable. We grow, and our music grows with us."

I finish off the last notes of *Control*, and nod to Dare. My heart thuds so loudly in my chest, I think he can probably hear it.

"Your turn," I say calmly.

Dare lets out a sigh as he gets up, heading for his guitar once more.

WHEN IT'S NEARING one am, we both decide to call it a night.

The hours flew by like sands in an hourglass. Slowly, but then all at once, poof. It was over.

We both stand in the foyer as I twirl my keys in my hand.

I look at Dare, yawning as he taps away on his phone.

I know I'm walking a tightrope with my own sanity, but damn it.

The need to *care*, to *give,* is so damn strong for this man who rips me apart and exposes me.

"I can give you a ride home," I offer firmly. It isn't a demand, or a command. Even though it should be.

No, instead, it is a *suggestion.*

Dare twists his lips as he looks up from his phone.

"Oh, it's all good. I called an Uber."

Panic floods me, along with anxiety, and Dare must sense it because his expression softens as he reaches out, running his fingers along my forearm *soothingly.*

"I can assure you, Matty, I have survived

plenty of Ubers in LA before you came along," he says with a smirk.

Maybe it's because it's one in the morning and I am tired, or maybe it's because the overindulgence of pizza, dumplings, and spicy pork has affected my brain chemistry.

"You will text me when you get home," I demand.

Dare haughtily grins, as he bites, "I don't think I have your number."

Little shit.

Is he fucking flirting *with me?*

My jaw tenses and I grit through my teeth, "Phone. Now."

Dare giggles.

Fucking giggles.

"Yes, sir, Batman," he chirps.

I scowl at his sarcasm, but I don't miss the way his touch lingers as he hands me his phone. It takes me all of two seconds to transfer my number to his phone, and when I hand it back, I, too, hold on longer than I should.

His fingertips against my skin make my blood rush, and his cocky little grin makes my palm twitch.

A blue sedan pulls up, and Dare smiles.

"Well, Matty, this is where I leave you," he says softly.

"The minute you get home," I growl.

Dare waves me off as he climbs into the car, and I am truly alone.

In the parking lot at one am.

I sigh in defeat as I leave the building, heading for my car.

By the time I get home, it's nearing two thirty, and I groan because I know I'll have to be up in four hours to get ready to head out for Karen Ingram's morning show.

Usually, I'm much more aware of my time, but the hours went by so easily, so fast, at the studio.

A part of me actually *enjoyed* playing my music with Dare, and helping him with his song. Though, I know he's not one hundred percent happy with the chorus, at least we were able to get something down that I think sounds pretty good.

I remove my shirt and pants, letting the cool air of my room kiss my skin. The trees sway in the wind, and I stretch along with their movement.

It's been years since I sat on that God awful couch in studio twelve, and my back is bitching.

It takes me no time to climb into bed, and just as I do, my phone chimes.

I reach to the nightstand, the light from my phone like a beacon.

I was abducted by aliens.

I smirk at Dare's text and his string of alien emojis, and let out a laugh.

Curling under the covers, I debate how to respond. I know I could just say 'k', or I could send a thumbs up, because I know he is safe and home.

But a part of me, one I haven't known for quite some time, rises from the ashes and decides to engage.

To play along.

Hopefully, they didn't probe you too hard.

I let out a giggle of my own, but Dare texts back quickly.

Not hard enough, I'm afraid. His emojis of winks and tongues sticking out, combined with his words make me blush, and my cock twitches.

Little shit.

I text him back an eye roll emoji.

Dare only texts me a bunch of alien faces and

eggplant and peach emojis with a *You're just jealous.*

Yeah, he's most definitely flirting.

I might not be up on all the emoji definitions, but I'm pretty sure eggplants and peaches are the very definition of flirting. Or is it... sexting?

I stare at the light of my screen, thinking about his words, about the other night when I watched the blond man trail his hands all over Dare's hips and thighs.

I want to say yes. That I am jealous, though I don't know *why*. Why the thought of anyone else's hands on his body makes my blood heat, why the thought of anyone *probing* his fine ass makes my jaw tense.

I close my eyes for a minute, if only to dispel the sudden rush of anger and anxiety that his words bring.

My cock throbs as I try to imagine anything but the thought of him being probed.

By my fingers, my tongue, my cock.

I groan in defeat as I sink my face into my pillow. My phone chimes, and I realize I've left him on read.

Did you fall asleep already or did the aliens get you, too?

I lick my lips as I respond.

Go to sleep, Dare.

I wait with bated breath for his bratty response, or perhaps, another thinly veiled innuendo about dicks.

But Dare does no such thing. He only sends a *Yes, sir*.

My jaw tenses and my cock throbs as I imagine those words escaping his lips, knowing how they sound.

Yes, sir.

I set my alarm, setting the phone on the nightstand, but I know it's no use.

Dare does not respond again, but his presence lingers in this space, in my brain.

There will be no sleeping unless I can cleanse him from my soul.

I let my hand travel down my abdomen, noting the hardness of my muscles beneath my touch.

My cock strains against my briefs, and I shimmy out of them with ease.

The velvet-like covers against my sensitive

cockhead feel good, despite the guilt forming in my brain.

I know I *shouldn't* think about Dare, especially not like this.

But I can't help myself, not when I know the things I do.

What his hair feels like in my grasp, tight and smooth.

What his hand wrapped around my wrist feels like, warm and soft.

God, I can only imagine what it would feel like wrapped around my cock, squeezing me, stroking me.

I know the way the shadows fall across his skin when he's tied up in ribbon, I know what his lips feel and taste like.

I can only imagine how beautiful he would look in my ropes, those perfect lips parted, waiting for a taste of me.

I know the deep, sexy sound of his voice when he's fucked up and the sweet, rambling energy that is the *real* Dare, and I know the beauty of his voice with nothing to dilute it.

I know his scent, the depth of his gaze, and the way he has somehow destroyed me and my fucking resolve.

I cannot deny Dare Wylde is truly a heart killer, and I am bleeding out.

I need a medic, stat.

I fight the urge to come, remembering the last time I came so close to release, with Dare grinding his cock against me, telling me he was going to make me *beg for it.*

For him.

But the fantasy is too hard to ignore when I bury my face into my pillow, and smell cheap cologne.

He was in this bed.

My bed.

The realization that he was so close, yet so far away, mingles with the ache in my soul, in my damn balls.

I roll over onto my knees, fucking my fist with steady rhythm as thoughts of Dare Wylde pull me underneath dark, undulating waves.

Not hard enough.

Yes, sir.

I'm going to fucking make you beg for it.

His words circle my brain, and I can't fight anymore.

Warm, thick release fills my fist as I curse his

name, and I groan in ecstasy and collapse against my satin sheets.

Every muscle in my body goes numb. My hips echo their dying thrusts as I come hard against the smooth sheets, breathing in his lingering scent like a blissful toxin. When I am finished, I groan as I roll over to open my night-stand drawer, snagging a couple of tissues, if only to clean up myself and the wicked wet spot that screams with the repercussions of my guilt.

My heart beats so loud in my chest, it is like a drum. When I am clean, I toss the tissues into the garbage can beside the table, then I curl my arms around the pillow that smells like Dare, and I whisper the words that come so easily as I drift off to sleep.

"Burning like a supernova
Burning bright, but so far,
Devour me, covet me
And I will bring you the moon, my wild star..."

CHAPTER 14

Dare

I stare at my ceiling, trying to convince myself I can see the stars instead of a white, boring ceiling with peeling paint.

Because as I lay here, Matty's bedroom is all I can think about.

Well, if I'm being honest, the bed I woke up in is not *all* I can think about.

I close my eyes as I work my cock, knowing the release will help me sleep.

Otherwise, I'll be tempted to stay up all night, trying to write and procrastinating sleep.

Mage Of Mercy's Control fills the space of

my bedroom, low enough it won't bother anyone else, and only I can hear it.

Matty's words dance in my brain along with his gravelly, roguish voice.

There are plenty of artists who are enhanced by technology, produced to sound good, but tonight, when I heard him sing in the studio—singing my favorite *Mage Of Mercy* song to boot—I couldn't deny that Matty is the real deal.

But if I'm being honest, it's not just his voice that makes my brain turn to mush, and it's not just the fact he's six foot four and built like a fucking brick house that makes my cock hard.

It's his attitude, his bite.

It's the sliver of moments where he cracks.

Where I can really see *him*.

Make no mistake, Mateo Starr is a dick.

But *Matty*... Matty is the man strumming away on a guitar, singing with raw emotion about needing control, about searching for satellites to call him home.

Or perhaps an alien to abduct him.

I know he said what happened between us would never happen again. That it *couldn't*.

But fuck, I want it to.

I want to kiss him, touch him, and fucking

eat him like a bowl of marshmallow fluff, and I want to lick that bowl damn *clean.*

The thought of licking Matty *anywhere* makes my cock wet, and I use my hand to spread the copious precum along my shaft like it's fucking lube. The damaged warranty expired brain cell that controls my cock latches on to Matty's dirty text.

Hopefully, you weren't probed too hard.

"Fuck me." I groan in the darkness of my bedroom, squeezing my thickness. My words ring out with resounding truth that only fuels my fire.

Fuck. Me.

The warmth of my hands melds with the moist feel of my precum and I know I'm not far off.

And because I'm clearly certifiable—as Matty says—I let my free hand travel up my chest to my neck, and I place my fingers around my throat.

In the privacy of my bedroom, at nearly three am, I have no reason to hold back.

So, I let my fantasy free, imagining Matty's hand around my throat.

I let go of my aching shaft, my hand and fingers wet enough with my own juices that I don't think twice about sinking a finger into my hole. The intrusion is sudden and causes a fresh blossom of moisture to form.

I shudder as my cock twitches, the cool air against the wetness and the tightness of my insides causing a deep moan to escape my throat.

It feels really fucking good.

My experience with men has been pretty limited to blowjobs, eating ass, and *once*, I hooked up with a dude at our launch party after we signed with Casualty Records, but I have to admit I was wasted, and as such, it didn't last very long by the time I managed to get my condom on. Two thrusts into the guy and I was toast, and he was, too.

But the thought of being *probed* by Matty, of letting him claim land no one else has, the thought of his fingers squeezing my throat while he stretches me...

I pick up my pace, my breath catching as my rhythm becomes more erratic, as the thought of his cock buried deep inside me while he *orders* me to beg for it fills my brain...

It's too much.

"Fuck me!" I groan into the side of my pillow as I come, diluting my ecstasy if only because I don't want to wake anyone else up and have them discover me like this.

Coming hard with my hand around my throat and a finger in my ass.

Finally, when I catch my breath, I open my eyes, noting the mess I've made. My cock is dripping, my waist and hips painted with my guilty pleasure, and I feel like I could pass the fuck out.

I reach for some tissues off my nightstand to clean myself up, if only because I don't want to wake up stuck to my damn sheets, and when I'm done, I close my eyes and listen to the faint sound of lyrics I know by heart.

Set me free, set me free
Baby, take control
Trap me, trap me, bury me
In your fucking soul
I don't want forgiveness, baby
I want to reap the seeds I've sown
Break me, take me, baby
I'm yours to control...

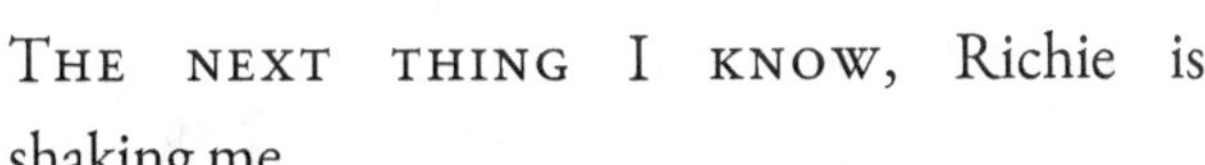

THE NEXT THING I KNOW, Richie is shaking me.

"Wake up, man!" he says, and I groan.

"Five more fucking minutes!" I whine.

"Not today! We've gotta head out in, like, half an hour. I already let you sleep late."

I whine again as I fight to throw my pillow at him, but he catches my hand mid-throw. The pillow falls between us.

"We've got a long day today. We've got the Morning Show," he says with concern.

"Morning Show?" I murmur as I sit up, wiping my eyes. My sheets fall around my hips, and I am startled to realize I'm commando under my sheets.

Shit, how the hell could I forget to put fucking pants on!

Richie doesn't bat an eye, though, and I'm more than thankful.

"Yeah, Karen Ingram's show. You *do* remember we have a show this morning..."

I run my hands over my face, nodding. "Yeah, of course," I lie.

Richie twists his lips. He looks like he wants to say something, but thinks better of it.

"All right, then hop to it," he says. "Or I'll have to sick Penny on you."

I groan, but wave him off. "Yeah, yeah. Give

me five minutes to shower and get dressed and I'll be down."

Richie grins, letting out a laugh as he heads for the door.

I STARE at my reflection in the makeup mirror. While I arrived to the studio in my new favorite sweatpants and a *Shrek* shirt that reads *Ogre On Board,* Karen's *team* had already selected an outfit for me to wear when I appear on their show.

I'm not one for suits, and as such, I'm not a fan of the black blazer and trousers with the gold shirt that draws more attention to my gut than anything I fucking own.

Richie, of course, is dressed similarly, but because he doesn't have an ounce of fat on his fucking body, the tight-fitting clothes only accentuate his fit figure.

I'm not jealous of my brother, but sometimes I wish we could have been switched at birth, and I could have been born *the pretty one.*

It's a lot easier to be confident about your looks when you look like Richie.

Thankfully, I was able to get the makeup and hair people to leave my hair alone, and at least that makes me feel like myself in this stupid suit.

Ines and Spike also sport daytime suits that cover their tattoos.

Looking up at the monitor, at the four of us sitting on Karen's couch, I can't help but think next to the three blond mice, I look like a fucking imposter.

Or Cinderella's salty cat, Lucifer.

Karen's voice pulls me from my melancholy thoughts and I realize she's talking to me, and of course I didn't hear her because I was too busy self-deprecating again.

"I'm sorry, can you say that again?" I say with a shrug.

Karen laughs, and Richie rolls his eyes. "You'll have to excuse my brother, his coffee hasn't kicked in yet."

I shoot him a scowl, but he doesn't falter.

Ines chimes in with his own sarcasm. "That's what happens when you stay out all night, am I right?" he teases, wiggling his eyebrows.

Spike laughs and shoots finger guns at the camera.

"Life of a *Heart Killer*, baby."

"Of course, and I completely understand!" Karen says with a giggle.

When all the laughing—my bandmates and the audience—settles, Karen implores me with her gaze.

"I was just asking if there is anyone special in *your* life. You boys have been the talk of the town lately, and viewers are just dying to know!" she says with a fake smile plastered on her face.

Fuck.

I wipe my sweaty hands on my knees, licking my lips as I try to think about how to answer her in a way that doesn't make me seem like a total loser.

Or a stalker.

"Uh, not... really," I say cautiously.

The crowd gasps.

Not helping the confidence here, ladies.

"I mean, it's not like I don't *want* there to be... someone. I just, uh..."

"I think what my brother means is that he's not in a rush. Like us, he's just enjoying the ride."

Riche pulls me close, and I take his lead.

"And it's been a *wild* ride," I say as I force a smile and wink.

The crowd and Karen laugh at my obvious

snarky allusion to my moniker and seem to take this as gospel, and move on to the next topic.

Our upcoming show.

Richie and Spike take over the conversations and drop our ticket information, and then we're off the air.

Once out of sight, I unbutton the top couple buttons of my gold shirt so I can breathe.

"You okay?" Richie asks as I pop a button off.

I hope I don't have to pay for that.

"I can't breathe in this fucking outfit," I say with a huff.

"I'm heading to craft services," Ines says.

"I'll come with you," Spike chimes in, leaving Richie and I alone.

I speed-walk toward the dressing rooms, wanting nothing more than to get out of this costume and put my comfy clothes back on.

"Somehow I don't think this is about the outfit," Richie murmurs.

I stop and look at him with disdain. "Really? Since when did you have time to get a shrink degree?"

Richie crosses his arms. "What is your deal, man? You've been a basket case since Sylvestro's."

"I have not!" I say like petulant child.

"Yes, you have. Something is going on with you." His eyebrows furrow as he takes a step closer to me.

I rub my neck, trying to re-circulate my blood flow from this tight ass shirt.

"You can tell me, you know," Richie says softly. "You used to tell me everything."

My heart breaks and I feel like an asshole.

How am I supposed to tell him something I barely understand myself?

What would I even say?

"I know, Rich. I just... don't think you would understand."

I don't miss the way his gaze falters or the frown on his face.

"Why? Is it a... guy thing?"

I've never been the type to remain quiet about my preferences. My brother was the first person I officially came out to, years before I came out to anyone else.

I wish I could tell him everything. About me, about Matty.

But something tells me now is not the time, and it's certainly not the place.

"Oh, my God! Richie! I didn't know you

guys were on the show today!" A sweet, melodic voice pulls both of our attentions.

But my attention doesn't fall on Hailee Starr, oh no.

Like a laser beam, it falls right on the tall glass of fucking water next to her.

Who is wearing his usual leather pants, black shirt with the sleeves rolled up. His chocolate brown hair is gelled back, and it gives him an almost debonair gentlemen look.

Gentleman of fucking hell.

My brother's entire demeanor shifts, and I don't miss the way his eyes light up when he looks at Hailee.

"Hailee! So good to see you," he purrs as he leans in and hugs her.

Matty meets my gaze, his expression as stoic as ever with his vast, starry gray eyes. He doesn't move an inch.

"Dare."

"Matty," I reply cooly, though I can't help but think about our conversation last night.

Or the seriously fucked up probing fantasy that followed.

My cock twitches and I shift my weight, not wanting to draw attention to these tight ass pants, just as Hailee squeals with excitement, her ombre curls bouncing like a basketball on hot concrete.

"I absolutely can not wait to see your show tonight!"

My burgeoning erection dies as all the blood drains from my body at her words.

"What show?"

Richie turns to me, his shoulders falling as he replies, "You know, the one at the Palace... at eight? It's been on the schedule for like six months."

I blink furiously, realizing I have no idea what he's talking about.

Panic sets in, because now I feel—and look—like an absolute idiot.

"Oh yeah, that one. Of course." I flash them with a forced smile. "How could I forget?"

Matty raises an eyebrow, just as Hailee *hits* him in the arm.

"You should totally come with me!"

I don't miss the way Matty snaps his head in her direction. "What?"

Hailee grins. "It'll be fun, just you and me. Like old times." Her blue eyes sparkle as she sways back and forth on her lithe legs, which are covered in opaque black tights with speckles of glitter.

Combined with her plum sheath dress and her gothic makeup, she and her brother look like they could pass as members of the Adams family.

"Yeah, it'll be a blast. We can even do something afterward... if you want," Richie says his demeanor cool and collected, but I don't miss the excitement in his eyes.

Matty glances at her, then at me, almost as if he is waiting for *me* to say something.

I clear my throat, glancing at Richie, who implores me with his gaze.

Oh, right, it's my band...

"Mateo, Hailee, we need you on set." A stagehand comes up, breaking our conversation.

Thank God.

Matty looks at me, then at my brother, and shrugs.

"I guess we'll see you later, then." His tone is cool, almost disinterested, and it takes a moment for his words to settle on me.

He's coming to my fucking show.

Tonight.

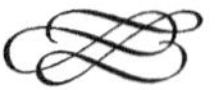

CHAPTER 15

MATEO

I STRAIGHTEN MY SUNGLASSES, even though where I'm going I don't *need* sunglasses.

Being out of the spotlight for the last few years, I've gotten better at going incognito, but I have to admit I haven't done many disguised outings since I moved back in with Hailee.

Honestly, I haven't done many outings at *all*, outside of our most recent trips to Fuku and Saint & Sinner.

The streetlights outside The Palace shine down on both of us, and the line outside the door is pretty long.

I turn to my sister, who, without all her makeup and gothic attire, looks like she could still pass as someone in their early twenties.

She's even forgone her usual extensions.

Fresh-faced with her hair pulled back in a bouncy brown ponytail and dressed in a *Heart Killer* tee and ripped blue jeans, the excitement in her eyes is unmistakable.

The sight reminds me of when we were teenagers going to shows, dreaming of becoming big stars ourselves someday.

Seeing her happy like this... I can't help but feel nostalgic, and also a little happy myself.

Though I know it isn't a good time with me, that has her all bright and beautiful.

I might not understand *what* she sees in Richard Wylde, but how can I judge her... or him... when I can feel her enthusiasm, her energy when he's around, like a living breathing entity?

"You don't really expect me to stand in line for an hour, do you?" I taunt her, sliding my hands into my jeans pocket.

I'm most known for my penchant for leather and black—in part because it's branding, and in part because it helps me *feel* more dominant—but I prefer jeans and converse to sweatpants or trousers when I'm dressing down.

Though Dare can pull off just about anything, it seems. Ripped jeans, gray sweatpants, form fitting suit slacks...

Hailee shoots me a smirk. "You really going to tell me you wouldn't wait in line for an hour to get a glimpse of Dare with his microphone between his legs?"

It is my turn to look appalled.

"Absolutely not!" I say deadpan, as she rolls her eyes.

"Uh huh, sure. Denial isn't just a river in Egypt, *Matty.*" She flashes me with a wink.

"Do not call me that," I snap, just as a security guard approaches us.

"Follow me," he says, and with that I am relieved.

My sister takes off like a rocket after him, leaving me no choice but to follow along.

We follow the man to the inside of the venue, to a private section on the left of the floor. There are only about ten seats in our section, already filled with individuals who must be of some importance, but that I don't recognize. Most of them, women.

Hailee immediately strikes up a conversation with the women beside us as the crowd starts to fill in, and I can't help but take in the sight of their sold out show.

When the lights go down, the crowd roars as the spotlights dance. Dare's voice carries over the loudspeakers asking his crowd if they are ready to be slayed. They roar in reciprocation as the lights flash, and some basic pyrotechnics go off.

Somewhere between the fire and the screeching guitars, Dare Wylde shows his true colors. He sings and he laughs with his crowd, tantalizing them with his infectious energy and a confidence that is undeniable.

And I realize as I watch him take the microphone stand between his legs, bending over as he cradles the mic itself, and his dark gaze catches mine, that I too am being slayed.

Because as I watch him command the audience and his stage, I can't deny the fact that despite my insistence, Dare Wylde has poisoned my blood.

With his bratty attitude and his fiery kiss, with his dramatic flair, his love handles, and so much more.

The realization strikes me and renders me frozen, like a glacier.

Because for the first time in a long time, I *long* to be broken.

To be destroyed by a *Heart Killer*.

The eternal moment ends only a second later, and before I know it, Hailee is tugging on my sleeve as the band leaves the stage.

I shake my head, realizing she's pulling me toward security again, and I follow her without question.

"Oh my God! You guys *killed* it!" She squeals as she abandons me and runs up to the band backstage.

Every one of them is covered in sweat, from head to toe. I fight the urge to stare at Dare, running a towel through his wet, dark hair, the sweat on his chest glinting in the low light.

"Thanks!" Richie says with a sheepish grin as Ines and Spike fist pump the air. "I'm so glad you guys could make it tonight."

Hailee gives him a hug and I stand off to the side, letting them have this moment, but also because I feel like a third wheel.

Dare wraps his towel around his neck. His

ripped jeans hang off of his hips deliciously, and I struggle to not look at his curves.

Everything about Dare is larger than life. His attitude, his personality, his fashion sense.

Like a supernova, exploding stardust in the dark

No planet could hold you

Because you are a wild star...

The words come to me easily, and a spark inside of me fuels. I want to tell him, to suggest them, but...

God, they sound so desperate, so awestruck, and....

I'm not entirely sure I can expose myself like that to Dare, let alone in front of my sister and his entire band.

So, I swallow my words as Dare's gaze catches mine.

"Hey Matty, the eighties called, they want their sunglasses back," he quips, flashing me with a devilish smirk, and I can't help the way my jaw tenses, or the way my palm twitches.

Or the way Dare cockily grins, because he *knows* just how to push my fucking buttons.

"Ah, yes, well, one needs shade when you're blinding everyone in a five mile radius."

I don't miss the way Dare's eyebrows knit together, or the falter in his expression.

Does he not understand how utterly bright he is?

"So, I believe someone said there would be drinks," Ines says as he elbows Richie.

Spike chimes in, nodding as he grabs a bottle of water from the pop up table next to him, downing it within seconds.

"Oh yeah, of course!" Richie says as Ines hands him a towel. "We should all go grab a drink and celebrate! The tour kicks off in less than a week! I can't believe we're almost there!"

Hailee nods in agreement. "I know, right? It seems like yesterday they announced all the acts, and in just a few days we'll all be performing the kick off show and then we're off!"

Dare tugs on the towel, covering his pale chest and nipples, and a part of me wishes he wouldn't cover himself as he is.

Richie, Ines, and Spike seem to have no qualms about exposing their tanned, solid and bare chests.

And then I catch Dare's gaze, the way it dips to them and then to the floor.

As if he is embarrassed, or ashamed.

Gone is the confident rockstar who owned the stage, and I realize that while Dare may know how to *command* attention when it comes to an audience, apart from the stage...

"Does Rosie's sound okay?" Hailee's voice brings me back to the here and now.

I tear my gaze from Dare, nodding as I take off my glasses and slide them in my pocket. "I suppose one drink won't hurt."

CHAPTER 16

MATEO

I TAKE my seat next to Dare as Hailee and Richie head for the dance floor. I've lost track of Spike and Ines, but knowing what I do of the drummer and the other bassist, I am certain they are flirting up a storm somewhere in the throngs of women surrounding the dance floor.

Dare carefully sips his beer, the same one he's been nursing since we got here.

After two drinks, I'm starting to feel a little more level.

"Why aren't you out there?" I inquire, curious. "With the rest of your band?"

Dare shifts in his seat next to me, his arm brushing mine lightly as he rolls the beer glass between his palms.

"Just not feeling it tonight, I guess," he replies, his voice soft and shy. I follow his gaze as it falls on his brother, and I see Spike and Ines arrive beside them.

Both men hang on their selected victims, as Richie and my sister smile and dance together, and I decide to put an end to this melancholy.

"You could have anyone in this club you want, you know that right?" I suggest, then take a sip of my drink.

Dare turns to me, raising an eyebrow. "How many of those have you had?" he asks, his voice loathsome and full of sarcasm.

I wave him off as I drain my drink. "It doesn't matter," I tell him. "The truth is the truth."

I don't miss the way his lips perk up at my comment, or the sparkle of mischief in his eye.

"Oh, so you're the only one who gets to be all bossy, is that it?"

"You're avoiding the truth, Darren."

Dare chews on his bottom lip, and I can't help but let my gaze flash to where he does so.

Remembering the feel of his lips against my own.

His neon orange and pink leopard print shirt makes his tattoos and the muscles of his arms stand out, and the shadows that fall on him from the neon lights behind us make him look wicked.

"And what truth is that, Matty?" he asks, his voice much darker, lower than before.

I lean closer, which forces him back into the tufted leather of the booth.

His dark gaze flashes to mine.

"That you are ten times the man any of them are," I state, my own voice cracking.

Dare's shoulders fall. "Yeah, that's kind of the problem," he murmurs, his gaze falling to my lips. His voice is full of cynicism.

"I think you misunderstand what I mean." I swallow harshly. "Spike, Ines... even your brother... they are a dime a dozen. Open up the pages of Rolling Stone, and you'll find ten, twenty rockstars just like them."

Dare looks down, and I do not think twice about grabbing him by the chin, startled by my own action. I drop my hand as his eyes widen.

"But there is no one like *you*." I move back,

needing the space. Because I fear if I do not, I will do much more than grab this man by the chin.

The softness in his voice cuts me like a knife. "You really think so?" he asks, almost as if he does not believe me.

I lick my lips as I consider my words carefully. "I know so, Dare," I tell him, and it is the truth. "Now get the fuck out there," I tell him.

I notice the grin forming on his face. "Is that an order, sir?" he asks, his voice dropping an octave.

I can't deny the way it makes my blood pulse, or my cock twitch.

"Yes," I say without thinking.

Dare only smiles and nods. "You too," he says as he stands up, offering me his hand. "You can't watch forever."

I debate telling him no. Debate staying here in the VIP, where I can safely observe the beautiful flame of Dare Wylde without getting burned.

But I don't want to sit on the sidelines of the game anymore.

I want to *be in it.*

Dare clears his throat as he says, "Unless you're *scared.*"

My jaw twitches and it is as if the response is automatic.

No one challenges me quite like Dare.

I grab his hand, and he pulls me up.

"Fuck no, I am not scared of a damn dance floor."

Dare licks his lips as he chuckles. "Then by all means, old man, show me your moves."

I follow Dare to the dance floor, where the rest of the band and my sister are.

I've never been much to enjoy clubbing, and prefer to dance with strangers, but the thought of dancing with anyone makes me feel uncomfortable.

The heat of the lights makes me feel flushed, and I start to think perhaps the two glasses of whiskey was a bad idea.

After all, it wasn't top shelf, and I'm far more accustomed to much better quality alcohol.

It doesn't take long for someone to gravitate toward Dare, just like I knew it wouldn't.

Dare's gaze flits to mine, almost as if he is asking permission.

As if he is *waiting* for me to tell him it's okay.

But I'm not sure it *is*.

As the music pounds around us, and bodies

bump and grind to the beat, I can't help but realize that we've been here before.

But somehow, this is *different*.

Because I don't want him to dance with anyone else.

I want him to dance with *me*.

I move forward, shaking my head, my gaze fixed on him.

"I'm good, thanks," Dare says over his shoulder to the dark-haired man behind him.

"Come on, bro, it's just a dance..." The man's voice is deep and tinged with drink. He slides his hand around Dare's waist, pulling him back.

Every part of me reacts to his touch, his attitude.

Dare wriggles a bit in the man's grasp, trying to remove his hand.

"I believe the man said, no, asshole," I bark as I come beside them.

Dare freezes, his gaze flashing up at me as the man who is *grabbing* him tightens his grip.

"Fuck off, I saw him first," he slurs.

I don't think twice, I just react.

Because clearly the alcohol has poisoned my

brain, and exposure to Dare has turned me fucking feral.

Or more or less, *my fist* reacts with the idiot's jaw, and he nearly falls over, and I realize too late I've fucked up.

Dare's pupils dilate and his mouth falls open.

And that's when I panic.

CHAPTER 17

O F ALL THE things I thought I'd see in my life, my teenage crush decking a man in front of me giving off *touch him and die energy*, was clearly not on my fucking list.

But the minute I see Matty punch the guy, I know one thing is for certain.

I'm in love with Mateo Starr.

I know it's batshit crazy and it makes no sense.

I'm twenty-three, he's thirty-nine.

I'm a mess, and he is all fucking order.

But fuck if I don't want to climb all six foot

four inches of this man like a damn tree because the man just punched a guy for me.

For me!

No one, man or woman, has ever thrown hands over me before.

How fucked up am I that I consider violence romantic?

My stupid, dumb heart grows three sizes bigger at the realization that *maybe* Matty feels this, too, this *thing* between us.

Even if he doesn't say it with his mouth.

His fist hitting that guy's face says it all.

"Fuck," he says as he shakes his hand, turning heel once more.

And I know he's going to run, but this time...

This time, I'm not letting him get away from me.

"Matty, wait..." I yell as I run after him.

Thankfully, he doesn't get too far from the dance floor before my hand is around his wrist once more. He stops, trying to break my hold, but I don't let him. I tighten my grip around his wrist and I pull him toward me.

"I'm sorry, I—"

I bring myself closer to him. In his jeans and

t-shirt, even with his sunglasses in his pocket, he looks divine.

While I'm used to the man who's always dressed for a funeral, there is something about the sight of him like this—dressed down, casual—that makes him feel more accessible, more relatable.

Younger, even.

His dark eyes peer at me, dancing with anxiety, and I can tell he *is* scared.

Because beneath the powerful, bitter, rockstar Batman persona of Mateo Star...

Matty is just a man like me.

Someone who *needs* the kind of love and acceptance he gives everyone else.

The words come easy to me, and I don't think twice about them as they slip from my lips. I've never felt as confident off stage as I do when I look at him.

"Do you want to, uh, get out of here? Go somewhere else?" I know the darkness in my voice is exposing me as the desperate man I am.

Desperate for him.

I watch as his bright blue eyes sparkle like stars in the night sky. I don't miss the glimmer of excitement that shines in them amid the neon lights as he tucks his shades in his front shirt pocket.

For a moment, I think he's going to snap, that he's going to pull away from me or deck me himself.

But he does no such thing.

His flesh against my palm is hot, and I can feel his pulse racing beneath my touch.

"Yes." It's a simple answer, but the weight of it is not lost on me.

Yes.

"Okay," I say, smiling as he pulls out his phone.

"I... think it is late, and we should get you home," he states, his voice gravelly, and all at once I think I gravely miscalculated.

He doesn't want to leave with me. Not like I thought. But I can't fight him, thinking perhaps maybe he *is* right. Maybe after this crazy day, I do need to just head home.

Matty pulls me through the crowd as my thoughts spiral, and by the time we are out of Rosie's, the limo is already waiting.

Matty opens the door for me, and I crawl in, feeling a sense of defeat as I try to wrap my head around everything's that happened.

How could such a great night go to shit so fast?

I performed my heart out this evening for *him*.

And now...

The door is barely shut before I open my mouth to speak, but the words don't make it out.

Because the second I open my mouth, Matty's lips crush mine with a startling ferocity.

I crumble like a well-baked cookie underneath his force as he grabs me by the throat.

His tongue slides into my mouth, and I note that he tastes bitter, like whiskey, but there is a smooth, sweetness that lingers on his lips.

But that's just Matty. He's bittersweet, and I love his taste.

I think I'm totally in love with him.

Fuck me.

"Matty," I sigh, as he pushes me into the cushions, throwing his leg over my lap. His hand on my neck tightens as he grinds his jean-clad cock against me, making me see stars as he bites at my lower lip.

I've only had one beer, but I have the feeling I could get drunk off of this man's kiss, off the way he touches me.

"Shut up," he bites, his tone edged in equal desperation as his hand on my hip travels to the waistband of my jeans.

The weight of him on top of me feels too good to fight, and I don't *want* to fight him.

Not when I can barely think straight because of the way he's touching me.

Like he wants to own every inch of me.

A deep groan escapes my throat as my last brain cell takes a nosedive.

"Make me," I breathe out, knowing it will be my death.

But death by Mateo Starr seems like a good way to go.

Matty's lips travel to my jaw, then my neck as he pops the button on my jeans, sliding his hand beneath them, the only thing separating my cock from heaven, a thin barrier of fabric. Though I'm more than aware that I'm harder than a slab of marble at the moment, I raise a shaky hand and test the waters.

I settle my hand on Matty's hip, tracing my fingers along his firm muscles, and the prominent tent in his fucking pants. His hand finds the slit in my boxers and within seconds, I can feel the warmth of his touch as he finds my cock.

The only sound thought in my brain is that I have died and gone to heaven. Because there's no other earthly explanation for why Mateo Star would be stroking my cock right now.

Right?

"Where are your words now, Darren?" he growls, his teeth nipping at my earlobe as he whispers in my ear. His voice is dark, confident, demanding.

"Fucking hell, Matty..."

His fingers tighten their grip. "You like this, don't you?" he bites, his fingers slipping through the precum of my weeping cock.

I close my eyes as my head falls back, his tight grip the only thing keeping me attached to the earth.

"Maybe..." I say, trying not to sound as desperate as I feel.

He chokes me just a little, and my cock throbs.

"There are no maybes, my little wild star. Only yes, or no."

My entire body melts into a puddle at his words.

My little wild star.

"Yes," I moan. "Yes, sir. I like this. Very

fucking much." My breath hitches, coming faster.

Matty freezes, and for a moment, I think maybe he's changed his mind.

That maybe the two drinks have metabolized out of his system and he's going to stop, like he did the other night at Saint & Sinner.

But instead, he tilts my chin up, forcing me to look up at him as he works my cock slowly, pumping, squeezing.

I'm so close... so damn close.

And almost as if he *knows*, he stops completely. My balls tighten and reflexively I thrust my hips, trying to keep the friction going, but Matty only shakes his head.

"Matty... please," I choke out as he removes his hand.

I need to feel his touch, I need to come so bad.

Matty grins evilly at me as he shakes his head. "No. Not yet," he says as he takes his now free hand, gliding it up my stomach. He presses his palm against my flesh, massaging my hips, and my cock throbs.

He's such a fucking dick.

"I need you to understand something first."

"Anything," I say, like the desperate man I am.

"This body..." He breathes the words against my ear as he removes his hand from my neck, bringing both hands to my hips and *grabbing* me. "This body is capable of great things," he says. His voice is dark, rumbling over the shell of my ear and sending shivers skating down my spine.

I swallow harshly as a bout of heat forms in my core. His legs pin me, and I can't move, my exposed cock twitching as a fresh bloom of wetness forms from the tone of his voice alone.

"This body..." he whispers in my ear, "...is a work of fucking art."

His right hand slides up beneath my shirt, fingers plucking at my nipple ring while his left grips my hip, squeezing my love handles, rubbing the extra bit of skin there that I've never been able to shake.

"Say it," he commands, and I feel like I can't breathe.

I want to say the words, but they are trapped in my throat. I look at him with pleading eyes. The way he's touching me, the sound of his voice makes me feel exposed in a way that has nothing to do with sex.

His bright eyes are full of heat, full of command. His fingers trace my skin, even the squishy bits, making my entire body warm.

"Matty, I—"

"Say it," he growls, like sexy Batman. "Know your worth, Dare."

He lifts his face from my neck, turning my chin to look into his eyes once more.

His thumb brushes my cheek and I nod.

"My body is capable of great things," I respond, my voice shaky.

"And?" he growls, his hand sliding down my neck, over my shoulder, trailing ever so leisurely down my chest. He traces the spot on my chest where the giant stitched heart lays.

"This body is a..." I swallow, feeling strangely on the spot, vulnerable.

I've performed for sold out crowds for the last year, given a hundred interviews—all disasters, nevertheless—but somehow these words are the hardest I've ever had to say.

"This body is a work of art." My voice is barely a whisper.

Matty holds my gaze.

"Good boy." His voice is stern and

commanding as he slides down my legs, to the limousine floor.

His hands push my legs apart, and he gazes up at me from between my legs, keeping eye contact as he takes my cock into the back of his throat in one swift motion, and I cry out with pleasure.

I don't know if I'm going to be able to hold it.

And when Matty rolls his tongue around my shaft, while massaging my damn balls, I can't.

My body locks up as I come and my hands find their way into Matty's dark hair, his fingers digging into the underside of my thighs.

I look up, through the skylight in the limo, and all I can see is the stars, and I feel like I am finally worthy of being one.

CHAPTER 18

Mateo

When the car stops, I feel like the world does, too.

Dare catches his breath, and I can still taste him in my mouth.

What have I done?

I can't even blame this on the alcohol. Two drinks may be enough to level me, but it is not enough to get me drunk enough to lower my inhibitions by any means.

I'm worried that any moment this bubble will break, and reality will set in, so I do the only thing I can think of.

I slide out of the car, and open his door.

Dare gazes up at me as he slides out of the limo, pausing for a moment as if he, too, is afraid to move.

And because I enjoy the torment, I implore him with my gaze, and my weakness takes hold.

"Let me walk you," I say, but it is not a command.

It is a wish, a prayer.

A sliver of hope that perhaps I can make this moment last a fraction longer before things get awkward.

I said this couldn't happen.

I promised myself I wouldn't *let* this happen.

But here I stand, before this magnetic man, bracing for the impact.

For the fall.

Dare nods as he looks up at me from underneath his dark lashes. "I'd like that," he replies, flashing me with a smirk.

And so, I walk him down the sidewalk, up the steps to his front door like a gentleman, and for the moment, it is enough that I can pretend we are just two people enjoying this fragile moment; the calm before the storm.

Dare pauses, and I know it is time to say goodbye.

"Well, I suppose this is where I—"

Dare leans in, wrapping one hand around my throat as he pulls me close, his soft lips pressing against mine, and all my resolve disappears.

I fall into his gravitational pull, opening my mouth once more for him, and his tongue probes mine.

I can still taste him in my mouth, and his kiss fills me with renewed desire.

I am powerless to resist this, resist him.

Dare irritates the living hell out of me, but he also illuminates me, terrifies me, and drives me fucking mad.

Perhaps it is I who is certifiable.

He breaks away from me, gazing up at me with glassy, dark eyes.

"Stay." He says the words firmly, with absolute clarity.

It isn't a suggestion.

It is a *demand.*

My dying heart aches to beat again at those words, but they frighten me.

More than anything.

My heart catches in my throat as I spiral out, debating what to say.

To stay or go.

Dare settles his hand on *my* hip.

I know I should push him away, but his touch is warm, and the air around us is cold.

His fire is addicting.

Like a wildfire spreading
Tearing down the forest of my heart
Destruction giving way to freedom
You are my wild star

"I know you're scared," he whispers, his pink tongue darting out to trace over his lips, and my entire body freezes at his words.

He tugs my hips gently, pulling me toward him, and I foolishly let him.

"I am not—" My voice betrays me as it shakes.

"But I need you to know something," he says softly.

Involuntarily, I lean into his space, seeking more of his warmth. Seeking the silky, smooth lips that silence everything else when they take control of mine.

"What's that?" I ask, my voice barely a whisper. I feel like I am on the edge of a cliff.

He smiles, and the sight is full of mischief. "Stay, and maybe you'll find out."

Little shit.

He shifts his weight, tossing some dark hair behind his shoulder.

"Besides, it's late, and my townhouse is a lot closer to the studio than your place is."

He isn't entirely wrong, and I can't argue with him about the logistics.

I look up at his townhouse, which looks so much smaller than anywhere I've been in the last twenty years.

It's a far cry from the woods, from the somewhat secluded property where Hailee and I reside.

"And you know no one else is home, and if I'm alone, well, something bad could happen." He grins. "You wouldn't want anything *bad* to happen to me, would you Matty?" he teases, his voice full of mischief and darkness.

Perhaps, it is because I have lost my marbles, or perhaps, it is because being around Dare makes me feel like I'm young again. Perhaps, the kid is rubbing off on me, infecting me with his sweet brand of chaos.

"Of course not," I say definitively. I look back to my driver, waving him off.

Dare opens the door, waving me in.

"After you, Batman."

When the door closes, it's like a switch inside me has been flipped. I take his face in my hands once more and I kiss him. Dare falters, falling back against the wall and bringing me with him. The sigh that leaves his throat sends a shiver racing through my spine.

His body softens under my weight as his lips move slowly against mine.

I bite at his lower lip, wanting to feel the in between.

His flesh between my teeth.

His silky hair between my fingers.

The moment between heaven and hell, between everything and nothing.

I've kissed Dare a few times, but none of those kisses felt like this.

Warm, raw, and all encompassing.

He pulls at the edges of my t-shirt as he leads me further into his house.

A part of me worries that his bandmates will be home at any moment, that they will walk in on us with our hands all over one another, lips frenzied and rushed as we both fight for dominance.

And the other part of me is thrilled by the thought of getting caught red-handed.

I follow him haphazardly to a bedroom, which I assume must be his.

I don't know where my shirt ends up, nor do I care at the moment.

All I care about at this moment is the warmth of his palms against my skin, the loud beating of my heart, and the feeling of free falling in darkness.

Dare fumbles with my jeans, and I slide out of them easily, letting them crumple to the floor. My movements are much more fluid as I unbutton his jeans, sliding my hands over his love handles once again, relishing in the feel of his skin beneath my palms.

I let my hands travel up his stomach, sliding beneath his shirt, and he removes it without haste.

For a moment, I steal a glimpse of him before me, dark hair a mess as locks fall over his pale shoulder, dark inky wings painted across his chest, steel rings glistening in the low light.

Dare pulls me back into him, his lips feverish

and warm against mine as he tightens his grip and we both fall to the bed easily with a thud. It isn't as soft as my mattress, but it isn't terribly uncomfortable.

I settle between his legs, breaking our kiss for a moment to look at him. In the shadow of his bedroom, beneath me, he looks absolutely perfect. His hair is splayed about his pillow, his pale skin contrasting with the dark sheets and covers. The curve of his thighs, and the slight indentation where his skin is trapped beneath the elastic waistband of his boxers, fresh pink marks from the constriction, causes my cock to throb.

His erection slides against my stomach as he arches his back, but his gaze is full of more than just lust.

It is full of something terrifying and beautiful.

Something that causes me to freeze.

"What is it?" I ask, worry building within me far too easily.

Dare looks like he wants to say something, but thinks better of it.

"You." His voice is barely a whisper. "I just... I never thought in my wildest dreams you'd be here, in my bed. With me. Like this." His voice, combined with the way he's looking at me is intoxicating

I'm not sure how to respond, or if I even can.

Dare leans up, pushing me back into his soft covers with one hand on my chest. He angles himself over top of me and I feel as if I can't move, even though I have all my faculties about me. All I can focus on is the heat of his palm right over my beating heart.

His push isn't rough or hurried, it's strangely gentle. As if he, too, is afraid of the fragility of this moment.

But the sight of Dare above me, of his dark hair falling in his eyes, of the muscles in his shoulders, of his kiss-swollen lips, resurrects a part of me I'd long since locked away.

And he is right.

I am *scared*.

Because the desire to give myself to this man, to *submit* to him, is fucking terrifying.

Giving anyone the power to break you is terrifying.

But I am powerless to fight his touch, and I fall back into his sheets, surrounded by him, his scent, his wicked grin, his warm touch.

My heart catches in my throat as he pins me

beneath him, cocking his head to the side, a devilish smirk playing on his lips.

This is it.

This is where I burn.

His sweet smile turns mischievous as he straddles me, pinning me, it seems, in a similar fashion as I had done to him only moments ago.

"That makes two of us," I murmur as he grinds his cock against mine. I bite my tongue, not wanting to give up so easily, long forgotten desires building within me, begging to be set free.

I don't want to give in. I don't want to lose control.

I want him to *take* it from me.

I can't be so easy, can I?

After all this time?

Fuck.

Dare smirks, his voice dropping an octave.

"Why did you hit that guy?" he asks.

I try to move, but his weight holds me like a stone.

On display before me, with all his tattoos and the dark look in his eye, it's impossible to refute the desire that he awakens within me.

Dare does not need ropes or ribbons to bind me.

"You know why.".

I fight to move, because submission feels so foreign.

I am always the one to *care* for my subs, to guide them, to rule them.

Not since I was Dare's age, have I engaged this part of me; the part I assumed died when my heart had been broken the *first* time.

Dare shakes his head. He slides his hands into the sides of my briefs, tugging roughly.

My cock twitches as his fingers stroke my defined muscles reverently, and then he slides his hand over my hip, grabbing the flesh of my ass with a tight squeeze.

"I want to hear you say it," he demands, and immediately, I understand exactly what he is doing.

Two can play at this game, wild star.

"Make me," I growl through my teeth, channeling my Dom voice.

I watch as Dare's pupils dilate, as something shifts in him.

He pulls my briefs down far enough for my cock to spring free. The chill air of the bedroom only solidifies the truth I can't deny.

His gaze implores mine, begging me to focus.

So, I look away, glancing to see him take out his thick, wet cock through the slit of his boxers once again.

"Is this what you want," he asks, his voice changing to something darker. Taunting me, tormenting me.

I look away, channeling my best Dare Wylde impression.

A devilish grin stretches across my face, and for the first time in a long time, I feel like switching.

"No," I bite, like a bitter brat, and it is like a weight has been lifted from my shoulders. It feels freeing.

"Liar," Dare says as he *spits* on my cock.

It takes an unnerving amount of concentration *not* to groan or look at him, especially, when it causes a fresh surge of precum to weep from my aching cock.

"Admit it, Matty. You were jealous," he growls.

Yes...

"Why would I be *jealous*?" I say petulantly.

Dare's warm fist circles my shaft, lathering his saliva with my own juices, and my jaw tenses.

"What reason would I have to possibly be

jealous of some asshole who doesn't know no means no," I bark.

"Because you want me. Admit it," he presses, and I grit my teeth.

"No."

"Liar, liar, your cock's on fire."

A moment later, he removes his hand, only to replace the touch with something harder.

His cock.

He thrusts against me, spreading the warm wetness, and I fight the urge to moan, because it feels so bloody good.

"I know you want me," he growls, grinding his hips and cock against mine. "That you want *this.*"

"Maybe." I shrug, looking away from him, trying to fight the grin that wants to spread on my face.

Dare bends down, brushing his cock against mine again as his lips hover above mine, inches away.

"There are no maybes, baby. Just yes or no," he whispers darkly, and my gaze falls to his lips.

Fuck.

Throwing my words back at me are you, wild star?

I know the rules.

After all, I made them.

"Yes," I grit through my teeth, my hips moving of their own accord as I fight to thrust myself against his thickness, seeking more of his hardness, more of the wet, rigid warmth that slides against me.

I struggle to keep the groan in my chest as he wraps his hand around the both of us. He takes his free hand and turns my face toward him, holding my neck with a strength that is absolutely heavenly.

"Admit it, Matty. You like this." He releases my neck, leaning back so I can get a full view of him straddling me, with both our cocks in his hand. "You like what I bring to the table."

I can feel the beginning of my orgasm culminating like a hurricane, and I know it won't be long if he keeps this up.

I don't want to give in, not this soon.

Dare releases his hold on me, and before I can find the words, he settles himself between my legs, grabbing my thighs, and *devours* me like I am nothing more than a piece of candy. He licks me from base to head as his fingers dance danger-ously close to my hole, and I squirm out of both shock and arousal.

A deep groan escapes me, and I cannot resist.

"Fucking hell, Dare," I hiss as he circles his tongue around my head, pressing into my wet slit as his thumb grazes over my sensitive skin.

I curse his name over and over.

Dare looks up at me from his place between my legs. "Admit it," he says, and then licking me like a goddamn lollipop, groaning and sucking like I truly am his favorite treat.

He stops and I curse him again.

Such a fucking brat!

"No," I groan.

Dare presses his thumb against my opening, just enough to inflict the most minimal pressure, and my cock throbs of its own accord. A strangled moan escapes me bitterly.

"Admit it and I'll *let* you come."

Fucking hell!

I breathe deep, trying to still the fire, my frayed nerves, and the truth that will undoubtedly be my undoing.

I cannot fight his command, not when I am this close to coming, this close to submitting.

The need to lose control, to lose myself, to be *free*... is too fucking much.

"Yes," I cry as he pumps my shaft with one hand, licking and nipping at my sensitive cockhead while he uses his thumb to massage my sensitive entrance, flicking, teasing me until I am nearly spasming from sensation alone.

It is a sweet sort of torment; that space between submission and dominance where I am no longer in control of anything.

Where my body speaks with a voice all its own.

"Yes, what?" Dare says, his cocky attitude as arousing as it is irritating. If he thinks he's going to get away with this...

I will punish him for this.

Mark my words, I will have my fucking revenge on Dare Wylde... one way, or another.

"Yes, I was jealous," I grit through my teeth.

Dare sucks on my swollen cockhead, pressing the tip of his thumb inside my sensitive hole just a hair, and I think I see stars. I'm so close.

So fucking close...

"And..." His velveteen voice taunts me between long, slow licks up and down my shaft.

He removes his explorative digit and leaves me writhing yet again.

I sigh, knowing it is the only way I will make it out alive.

"I..." The words catch in my throat, and I am unsure if I am making a grave mistake.

I suck in a deep breath and breathe the words that will utterly destroy me. Because I'll never be able to forget their truth, and with truth comes harsh reality.

"Yes, Dare. I want you," I growl. "But right now, I want—" I twist and buck beneath him, seeking whatever sensation I can get, chasing after my ecstasy.

"Tell me what you want, Matty," he taunts me.

I huff out an angry, frustrated growl as he licks my leaking cock, his warm tongue making me see stars.

"Right now, I want to fucking come, asshole."

Dare chuckles darkly. "You didn't say please..." he says brattily, licking me until another angry moan escapes my lips.

I know what he wants, and so close to release, I can't fight him.

I can't fight myself, or the words.

"Please," I beg.

I don't miss the way his lips turn up in a smile, or the light in his eyes at my words.

He grins confidently, and my breath catches in my throat as he stops, making my cock throb.

"Fuck!" I curse as another desperate plea escapes my throat.

"Please, Dare... I can't, I—" My voice breaks with the need, the desperation that clouds me like a poison.

"Told you I'd make you beg," he says darkly before devouring me once more, taking me all the way to the back of his throat in one fell swoop.

I come without warning, my entire body tensing as my orgasm rips through me like an earthquake.

I reach out, grabbing onto sheets and pillows as I shudder and pulse, as I submit to Dare's sweet, sweet, chaos.

To *him*.

His deep groan pulls me back from the heavens, and when I open my eyes, I can see his hand, wrapped around his cock, his own release frothing down the sides of his fist.

I watch hazily as Dare swallows every drop of me.

When he gets up, I feel empty, but also strangely whole.

My eyelids flutter shut, and I hear the sound of running water. A moment later, I can feel his weight on the bed, and the rough feel of a towel against my soft, deflating cock.

"You don't have to—" I murmur, but Dare's lips silence me.

"I know, but maybe I want to." His touch, the way he *cares* for me, is different than before. It's still warm, but it's softer.

I kiss him back weakly as slumber threatens to pull me under.

He breaks our kiss, and a moment later, I feel the tightness of my silky briefs caging me once more.

Warmth surrounds me as Dare pulls my body against his.

His hair tickles my skin, and I let out a euphoric sigh of relief.

I can't remember the last time anyone *held* me.

Edward tried to, in the beginning of our relationship—our contract—but I had always felt like it was *my* job as a Dom to care for him, and as such, I didn't *need* anyone to care for me.

Intimacy, love... all of that was wrapped up in the trust my subs gave me, in the trust I gave them.

But the moment Dare drapes his arm over my hip, burrowing his face into my shoulder, I feel a sense of relief.

I *like* it.

So, I don't *fight*. I'm too tired to fight.

Dare's soothing, dark voice lulls me into a peace I've never known as he sings.

"I can feel your light, your shimmer
No matter how far
I'd travel the universe
Just to get a glimpse of you, wild star."

CHAPTER 19

DARE

"EARTH TO DARE!" Richie calls, pulling me from my daydreams. I note his expression as he nods at the amp at the edge of the stage.

"Oh, right, sorry," I say as I head over to help him with the equipment so we can get ready for sound check.

I still can't believe tonight kicks off our tour.

The last few days have been nothing but craziness as we all tried to cram in as many appearances as we could on practically every show that would take us.

Which meant rehearsals were sporadic at best, which means I haven't seen Matty since...

Since I woke up curled around him like a damn facehugger.

Or a stage five clinger.

Real smooth, Dare.

I'd wanted nothing more than to stay in bed with him, wrapped around him like a monkey, but I could see in his eyes he was already freaking out, and I didn't want to add to his meltdown.

I'm not an idiot, I know Matty's dating history, just like most *Mage Of Mercy* fans do, but I'm pretty sure a blind man could tell his venomous tone, his bite...

It's a defense mechanism.

I don't know the details, but I know you don't just get over a guy you were with for five years.

A guy who is all over the Internet right now with some rising star model who looks like he could use a cheeseburger. Or two.

And then *Penny* showed up, which did not help my game whatsoever.

I'd walked him outside, to where the limousine was waiting creepily, like it'd been there all along.

I didn't want him to go, but I knew he needed to.

And almost as if he could *feel* my spiraling thoughts, he leaned forward, kissed me softly, and told me goodbye.

And I haven't seen him since, thanks to our clashing schedules, and every time I *think* about texting him, I end up writing a fucking dissertation and then erasing it because I don't want to sound like a fucking stalker.

But today I *will* see him.

Because it's the summit tonight. It's our first show of the *Pillars of Rock* tour, and he'll be here for sound check, just like all the other acts.

I drop the amp next to my microphone as Ines and Spike bring out the guitars.

"You good, bro?" Richie inquires once we set everything down.

"Yeah, of course," I reply, even though I feel a little on edge.

We've played a lot of places, big and small, but never a *stadium*.

Though I think if I think about it too much, I'll jinx myself, so instead of focusing on the biggest show of my life this evening...

"You just seem a little..."

"What?" I ask as the sound check guys call out for us to tune.

"You have been walking around with your head in the clouds for the last four days, man. It's like you are somewhere else completely. I just want to make sure you're good, you know?"

I sigh in exasperation. When did my brother become the *talk our feelings out* guy?

"I just have a lot on my mind, you know, with the tour."

Spike brushes against my side as he messes with some chords and wires.

"We're all nervous about the tour, Dare," Richie says with a sigh of his own.

"And then there's the next big hit," Spike grunts.

"What's that supposed to mean?" I ask.

Spike shrugs. "We haven't worked on the *Slayer* album in weeks, man. All I'm saying, is we need to get our shit together, you know?"

I shoot my brother a look, and he holds his hands up.

"He's not wrong, Dare. Every time we *ask* how Wild Stars is coming, you tell us we'll be working soon, but..."

I purse my lips as his words settle on me. He's not wrong, but then again, how could I tell them—any of them—that I was struck with the worst case of writer's block—until recently, that is.

"We will. We've got the next three months on the bus, that's plenty of time to work on the album," I say.

After the last week, I think I've got more than half the lyrics out to a point where I like them, but I'm still missing something.

Richie turns on his guitar as one of the engineers signals our test.

"I hope so, Dare," he says, and I don't miss the sadness in his eyes.

I promise myself that once everything is settled—this show, getting my shit packed, and of course, my impending insanity regarding the one and only Mateo Star—once we are on that bus, I'll get to the bottom of whatever is bothering my brother.

I hang out in the alcove, watching Geo rock his sound check. I don't know the guy well, but I like a few of *Gravedigger*'s songs. But I can't deny that the guy puts on a good show, and definitely commands a presence of his own.

And just as he wraps up the last notes of his last song, I see them.

Mage Of Mercy.

Matty walks out in a pair of ripped, darkwash jeans, a heathered black shirt, and a pair of black converses, while his sister dons a similar outfit, except she's traded jeans for shorts that show off her long, lithe legs. Her hi-top converses and her long bouncy ombre waves only add to the youthful look she has.

I watch as they breeze through their sound check, hiding in the shadows.

Matty strums away on his guitar, his stance dominant and commanding, even though there is no audience to woo.

But I have a feeling that's just who Mateo Starr is. He's a force of nature, like a supernova.

And as I watch him, I can't help but get swept up in his performance. His voice, the way his fingers dance along the frets, and the way he commands his stage.

Fuck.

I know it's only been a few days, but the one thing I've realized during that time is that I know without a doubt what I *want.*

I don't waste any time the moment he tears off the stage, and I practically sprint over to him.

"Hey," I say, pulling his and Hailee's attention.

Matty stops, and so does Hailee.

"Dare..." He clears his throat, looking from me to his sister. "I didn't see you there."

Hailee nods as she looks around me. "Your, uh... brother around?" she asks nonchalantly, but I can see the glimmer of interest in her eyes.

Something is definitely going on between them. Maybe that's why my brother has been up my ass the last few days, because he's avoiding his own shit. That would be classic Richie.

Maybe I'm not the only one wishing on a Starr.

"I, uh, think I saw him in the break room a little bit ago," I reply with a polite grin.

Hailee nods. "I'm kinda hungry anyway, so, uh... I will catch up with you two later?" She says the words softly, almost as if she is afraid they will break.

Matty nods. "Of course."

I watch as she walks off, her ombre curls bouncing behind her.

This is it.

This is quite possibly the biggest moment of my life.

I shift my stance as I slide my sweaty palms in my black jeans pockets, glancing up at the tall glass of fucking water in front of me.

God, he is so fucking fine.

"So, I was… uh… thinking," I say, clearing my throat.

Matty crosses his arms, raising an eyebrow. "Should I alert the press? Or should I stand by with a fire extinguisher?" he bites out, but there's an edge of something less bitter than usual.

Almost as if he is *teasing* me.

Which only fuels my fire.

"Well, that depends on your answer, Matty," I quip, flashing him with a smile.

"I told you not to call me that," he growls, shifting his stance in the shadowed alcove, which only puts him closer to me.

My heart feels like it's in my throat, and I am acutely aware of the space between us. The sliver of space that is slowly closing.

"I, uh, want to ask you something," I say, his gaze making me feel warm.

"Is that so?" His voice is calm and cool.

"Uh huh," I reply, fighting the urge to lean in

and kiss him, to push him up against this wall and—

Focus, Dare!

"English, Dare," he taunts me.

I take a deep breath, steeling what little resolve I have, because being in this man's proximity melts my fucking brain.

I have no goblins working the gears when Matty is around.

I am all instinct, all impulse.

"So, I was thinking..." I say, reaching a hand behind my head, playing with my hair, if only to quell my nerves. "That maybe we could like... hang out after the show tonight? Grab something to eat or—"

"I can ask Haileee if—"

"No, I, uh... I mean just you. And me," I say, nibbling on my bottom lip.

My heart beats so loud I think it's actually echoing in the space, but a quick glance shows it's just the damn sound engineers messing around.

Matty's eyes narrow at me and his jaw tenses.

"Like a date, you mean?" His voice is solid and unwavering, and I feel like a victim of kidnapping or something.

Unsure if my captor is going to beat the shit out of me, or if we're just going to chat about the fucking weather while I'm tied to a chair.

Although, I wouldn't mind being tied to a chair and tortured by Matty, fuck.

Focus! Dare!

I try to feign nonchalance, but I fail miserably as I let out a nervous laugh.

"Oh, uh… well, it doesn't *have* to be a date. I mean, if you don't want it to be. We can just, uh, like, hang out and maybe jam a bit? Work on the song together, or—"

Matty's lips turn up in the corner just the slightest, making me blush.

"I have conditions," he says stoically, and I blink.

That wasn't a no.

"Oh, uh… yeah… of course you do. Uh—"

"I pick the place," he says matter-of-factly.

"Yeah… yeah, sure," I reply, nodding so much I think my head may fall off. "Whatever you want. I'm totally at your mercy." I realize the moment I say the words, I have sealed my fucking doom.

Matty grins, and the sight makes my body

flush with heat, my cock standing at attention once more.

Matty moves just the slightest, but the motion puts me back against the wall.

He leans his arm out casually, bracing against the wall so he can loom over me like a villain in a romance novel or some shit.

But I like it.

I like how he makes me feel like I never know what is going to happen with him.

He could kill me or he could kiss me, and honestly I'm down with either.

Maybe both, if I am being honest.

"You will meet me at loading dock C-7 at nine-thirty." His voice is clear as a bell, and solid.

I nod as he leans his face close to mine; so close, I can feel the heat of his breath, smell the overpowering scent of eucalyptus and sexy shower gel, and I sigh.

Like a damn swoon-worthy heroine.

"Yes, sir," I agree, licking my suddenly dry lips.

Matty grins and removes himself from my space.

"Good boy. I'll see you later, Darren."

And with that, he walks away from me, leaving me hard and wanting all over again.

He said yes.

I wait until I'm certain he is gone before I fist pump the air and whisper a resounding victorious *yes.*

Tonight is going to be the best night of my fucking life! I just know it!

CHAPTER 20

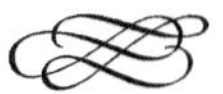

Mateo

This is a terrible idea.

A date.

With the man I haven't been able to get out of my head since the other night.

Four days ago, I woke up in Dare Wylde's bed, with our bodies entangled together, and I realized a startling revelation.

I was no longer *falling* in love.

I'd hit the pavement, with Dare.

And that was, at the time, something that terrified me.

It always starts with a kiss, and no matter

how hard I fight love, I am its biggest fucking victim.

I *switched* for him, and the magnitude of that alone told me everything I needed to know.

And my first reaction had been to run.

Run far away from the sun because fire was catching.

I'd worried I'd fucked everything up.

And over the last few days, I thought a lot about what happened between us the other night.

But in all honesty, I know it wasn't just the other night.

It was a multitude of little moments, ranging from irritating as fuck, to sweet as hell, and everything in between.

Somewhere in the middle of my bitterness, I found something delicious.

Something *perfect*.

I'd thought so much about what I wanted to say these last few days, but the moment I saw him, nothing came to mind.

Dare Wylde renders me speechless, it seems.

Then, he bravely stared me down this afternoon with his own brand of dominance and asked me on a fucking date, like we were two high schoolers and there was a dance on Friday night.

And like I had the other night, I gave in easily.

Too easily.

The moment I said yes, I knew exactly where I wanted to take him, and I knew exactly what I needed to do. What I needed to say, and exactly how to say it.

Dare approaches my car, hands in his pockets, looking as devilish as ever in his black jeans and a neon purple tank top.

"Sweet ride," he says with a whistle as he approaches me.

I lean against my car, taking in the sight of the way his jeans hug the curve of his ass, stifling my own desire.

I need this night to go well.

I need him to understand how much he means to me.

I open the passenger door for him. "Get in."

Dare rolls his eyes, "So fucking bossy."

The tone in his voice is not angry or irritated by any means, and I don't miss the way he grins, either.

The way he responds to my Dom voice is

obvious, and I garner he may have some natural dominant tendencies of his own underlying, but is he truly capable of what I *wish* him to be?

Just because I *want* him to obey, doesn't mean he will. That he will understand the depth of what being *mine* means.

But I know, as I look at him in my car, and we drive up the winding, dark road, that I want him to be.

I want Dare to be *mine* in every sense of the word.

"Should I be concerned, we haven't seen a streetlight in like an hour," he says, flashing me with a grin.

I focus my attention on the road.

"We are almost there," I reply as the radio plays Geo's newest single, *Heaven Sent.* His words about finding an angel are somehow soothing and irritating at the same time.

Dare leans over the console, his voice darkening. "Are you taking me to your Bat Cave?" he says with excitement.

It is my turn to roll my eyes and reconsider my plan.

Only for a moment, anyway.

"Something like that," I respond as I make

the turn down a dirt road, finally coming to a stop on the edge of a grassy knoll.

I shift the console up, giving us both a bit more range of motion as I change the station to something more ambient.

"Stay," I order as I open my door.

Dare grunts out a petulant response, but it is barely audible.

I open the trunk, pulling out my blanket and a cooler full of drinks, and of course, some take out from Mila's.

"Wow, what is this place?" he asks as I open his door, motioning for him to join me on the grass.

I waste no time rolling out the blanket across the ground, plopping the cooler down in the corner to hold it down.

"After you." I motion for him to take a seat.

Dare chews on his bottom lip, but does as I say without too much of a fight.

I take my spot next to him, feeling more nervous than I have in a long time.

I've only been here, in this position, twice. Once with my high school boyfriend, Craig, and once with Edward, before we moved in together.

The levity of that fact is not lost on me as I

watch Dare lean back on his elbows, looking up at the sky.

"It's so... pretty," he breathes out in awe, and I can't stop looking at him.

At the way his dark hair falls over his shoulder, at the way his dark eyelashes frame his pale skin.

"Yes. You are," I say like an absolute love struck idiot.

But it's the damn truth.

Dare turns to look at me, and I cannot help myself as I reach out, and cupping my hand behind his head, I pull him toward me and bring his lips to mine.

He kisses me with ease, melting into my hold like butter on a hot skillet.

Gone are the words I wish to say.

The truth I need to tell.

Because when I pull Dare to the blanket with me, when he curls into my side as I point out stars, somehow everything seems *right.*

And I don't want to ruin the moment with my truth.

I just want to hold his warm body a little longer.

And when he looms over top of me, pressing

his warm lips to mine, I become one with the stars, myself.

Emotion clouds my judgment, making me hazy.

Dare pulls me close, leaning back so that he is beneath me. I can feel his hardness, and I respond to it with a groan as I pin him beneath me, relishing in the feeling.

His hands travel over my ass and he looks up at me with bright eyes, his skin flushed with heat, his lips swollen from my kisses.

God, he is a constellation all his own.

Dare licks his pouty lips as he breathes out the words that are my utter undoing.

CHAPTER 21

DARE

MY WIRES CROSS, and I'm not sure I'm making sense.

I want to say I love you.

But all that comes out is "I want you," and it comes out sounding like I can't breathe.

It isn't untrue.

I *do* want him.

I want to write songs together and jam, and I want to piss him off, and I want to make him crumble like a cookie beneath me, and I want to gaze at the stars in his arms, and wake up with him wrapped around me.

I want Mateo Star to be *mine.*

Matty kisses me, speaking a language only our bodies seem to know.

He trails his fingers down my side, gripping my hips as I thrust my cock against him.

"I know," he whispers.

Underneath his weight, in the middle of nowhere, with him on top of me, I can't deny that everything feels perfect.

He feels perfect.

And with my brain goblins on strike again, I don't think twice about what I say next.

Because when I'm with Matty, I'm not afraid of fucking anything, least of all my own thoughts.

"I want you to fuck me," I breathe out, taking his lips against mine.

"Dare..." His voice drops, and I can hear the fear in it.

"Please," I beg.

His cock throbs against mine, and his grip tightens on my hips.

"It's not... It's not that simple, Dare," he replies as he leans back, taking his weight off of me.

What?

Panic sets in.

Did I say something wrong?

Did I miscalculate?

Matty adjusts his cock, and I lean forward, anxiety spreading in me like wildfire.

"Matty, what's—"

"I knew this was a bad idea," he murmurs, and my heart breaks.

"What?" I can feel the tears starting in my core, working their way up to my eyes.

"I thought..." I stammer, trying to find my words as old insecurities and memories push forth. Of the women and men who didn't *want* me the way I wanted them.

"I thought... the picnic... the stars... the making out... I mean, like, this is the most romantic shit anyone's ever done for me. So, I thought—"

The air is cold and I can feel my tears prickling my eyes.

Matty sighs, running his hand over his face. "It's complicated."

Complicated? How is sex complicated? We've already slept together! Well, in the literal sense, and we've fooled around. How can this be complicated?

"Whatever, I get it, I—" I stand and he does, too.

"Darren..." His voice is strained.

"Just give me a chance to explain, please," he pleads as I give him my back, if only so he can't see me cry like a fucking baby.

"It's fine," I reply, my voice shaking.

"Fuck, now you're crying. I can't—" His voice takes on an edge that only makes me feel worse. Great, now he's mad.

"Dare, will you just listen to me, damn it!" he says.

I turn to look at him, and I can see the pain etched all over his face.

Pain I caused because I'm an idiot and ruined everything.

"I just have... needs," he says, his voice full of pain.

I turn to face him, noting that he's already cleaning up our spot.

Guess the date's over because I fucking blew it.

"What kind of needs?" I snap, crossing my arms.

Matty sighs as he packs up the trunk, then opens my door.

He motions for me to get in, and I think about not doing it.

But if I don't, I'll be stuck out in the cold.

Fucking weather.

Matty turns the car on, but there is no music. Just the utter darkness and silence.

"Sex is an intimate thing for me," he says firmly.

"Um, yeah, that's kind of the definition, there, Matty. It's intimate for *everyone,*" I bite, looking out the window.

"I need your explicit consent," he says.

"Pretty sure me asking for it, *is* my consent, sir."

"In writing," he says, and the car gets quiet.

"Like a... a NDA?" I ask. I'm not stupid, I know plenty of people have them, but I never thought I'd need one.

"Yes," he says as he swallows harshly. "Among other things."

I narrow my eyes at him. "What kind of other things?"

The car grows quiet once again, and I think he's purposely avoiding my question when he says, "Prep testing, a status of our arrangement, your safe word, and a list of hard and soft limits, of course." The way he says the words is methodical. Removed.

But I can see the way his jaw tenses, and the way his lip quivers, and I know whatever this is—it's monumental.

"Testing, right. Yeah, of course, I mean, that's like, the responsible thing to do, when you're like, dating someone, right?" I start to ramble.

Are we even dating?

Are we just fucking around?

What are we?

I don't even know.

Shit!

"Safe word, I don't even know what that is, and limits? I don't fucking know, I've slept with like two people... okay, three... four, probably, if you include you in that mix... And, I mean, what are your *limits?*"

Matty's arms tense as he stares at the road, his jaw clenched.

"I can't disclose that without a contract, Dare."

Oh.

Oh.

Realization hits me at what he is getting at, and his words from before, echo in my brain.

I can't legally tell you.

"So it's a kink thing." I say nodding slowly. "Like Fifty Shades of Gray or some shit? Did your, uh, other... Did you make Eddy Spaghetti sign a contract?"

The car comes to an abrupt stop at a stop sign.

Matty is only inches away from me, but it feels like a canyon.

"What did you call him?"

I swallow harshly. "Eddy Spaghetti. Because he did that pasta commercial, you know... before he was famous."

I watch the vein over Matty's eye twitch.

Well, it was good while it lasted, Dare.

I hope Richie throws a nice funeral.

"Yes," he says quietly, the sound of the engine only accentuating the silence between us.

Neither of us speaks until we come to my driveway.

I open my mouth, but he only gets out of the car, opening my door like the perfect date.

The perfect date I fucking ruined with my damn cock.

I get out, and he walks me slowly down the sidewalk.

"I'm sorry, Dare," he says softly. "I just... This isn't easy for me." His voice is barely a whisper. "I don't know how to do this." He stops in front of my door.

"Do what?" I ask, my voice sounding tired.

"This," he says, swallowing harshly as he motions between us.

His eyes glisten as he whispers words I know all too well.

"You prayed for my love, you begged for my heart...

And it is time to reap what you've sown...

All you have to do is sign the dotted line, baby." His voice falters and I can hear the sadness in it.

And as I look at him on my porch, I think I finally understand.

This is who Mateo Starr really is.

A man who needs to be in control in all aspects of his life.

A man who desperately wants someone else to take it from him.

Can I be that person?

Am I capable of being what he *needs*?

Because I know he's everything I need, everything I want.

Fuck, he's *everything* I never thought I *could* have.

I was nervous before asking him on this date, but now?

Now, I feel like I really am certifiable.

Because I've never taken a leap of faith, quite like this.

This could blow up in my face, or it could be the best decision of my damn life.

"Okay," I agree, my breath catching. I don't miss the shift in his eyes, the way his muscles loosen.

"Okay?" the concern, the hope in his voice is not lost on me.

I nod.

And when he presses his warm lips to mine, I can't help but whisper the words that will seal my fate forever.

"Give me your control."

CHAPTER 22

Mateo

I keep looking over the contract Dare signed, half expecting it to dissolve into thin air.

With the exception of his testing, everything has been filled out and then some. Some areas have been highlighted and tabbed with post it notes, Dare's messy writing asking questions or making comments.

I swipe my phone up, dismissing the notification as a knock on my door pulls my attention.

I turn to see it is my sister.

"Hey, a bunch of us are headed out to get

something to eat, you want to come with?" she asks.

I nibble on my lips and she catches my gaze.

"You okay?" she asks.

"I should be asking you that question," I murmur as she enters the dressing room.

"You know traveling always gets to me," she says softly, coming to sit beside me.

"Mhmm. And Richie Wylde has *nothing* to do with your mood as of late."

Hailee shrugs, but she does not deny it.

"Same way *Dare* has nothing to do with yours."

I can't help but chuckle at the reality of the situation.

"Must be something in the Wylde DNA."

Hailee laughs, and I can't help but laugh, too.

"You really like him, don't you?" she asks softly.

A sense of relief falls over me, and I can't refute her truth.

I look at her, feeling exposed in an entirely new way.

"I think I might be in love with him, Hailee."

Hailee purses her lips. "Love is a good thing, Mateo. It's not all heartbreak and sad songs."

Something tells me I'm not the one she's truly trying to convince.

"Sometimes, you just need to take a leap of faith." She forces a smile.

"Is it you who can't jump, or him?" I ask, not beating around the bush.

"Me," she replies quietly.

I wrap my arm around her, pulling her close. "You deserve someone who makes you happy, Hailee."

She sighs, her shoulders falling forward. "So do you, Mateo." She gives me a half smile.

"I'll make you a deal," I say as she smiles. "I'll jump, if you do. That way, if I end up in a ditch, you'll be there, too," I tease with saccharine sarcasm.

Hailee smiles, punching me in the arm. "Way to kill the mood, *Matty*," she bites and the moment escapes us.

"Do not call me that," I snap. "For fucks sake."

Hailee stands, smiling sweetly. "I don't know, I kinda like it." She turns on her heel and heads out the door without allowing me anything to counter that parting shot.

I STARE at the text on my phone, while I wait outside Dare's door.

When he opens it, I can't help but feel awestruck.

For one, he's shirtless, wearing those damn gray sweatpants that hang off his love handles deliciously, but his hair is wet and he smells like a mixture of cheap cologne and lavender soap.

It's a heady concoction, honestly.

"Matty, hey…" he says with surprise shining in his eyes.

"You have not returned my texts," I say firmly, the warmth of the pizza box hot against my hand. I see his pupils dilate as he looks to the box in my hands.

"So you thought you'd do a welfare check on me, is that it?" he nips.

"Something like that," I reply, a grin forming on my face. "May I come in, Darren? Or is there a reason you are keeping me and this delicious pizza outside your hotel room?"

Dare chews his lip. "I just... wasn't expecting a visitor," he says as he moves aside for me to enter.

"Did you read your contract?" I ask, wasting no time as I set the pizza down on the dresser and my duffel bag on the chair in front of the desk. I unzip it methodically, so that I have everything I need at my disposal.

His room is a mess, clothes and belongings strewn across the furniture, and he's got the television on, but it's on mute.

"Yeah, of course," he says nervously.

"Then you would know that under paragraph three, line one, failure to respond to your dominant—me—in a timely matter, will result in my coming to check up on you. To make sure you are safe, of course."

Dare watches me with interest, following my movements with his dark eyes.

"Uh huh. And failure to do so means I get punished, right?" he says with a grin, as he stalks closer to me.

Well, fuck.

I played right into that, didn't I?

Perhaps Dare is smarter than he looks.

I stand my ground, making no motion to

betray my sudden panic to him.

I need to remain in control, of course.

"That is correct. But first, you will tell me *why* you did not respond."

Dare shrugs, running his thick fingers through his hair. "I just... sometimes I get in my head about stuff. I've been working on Wild Star, and, like, I'm just... not that I'm *worried* about my test results or anything, but, like, I just don't do good with waiting." He blows out a frustrated sigh. "I don't like not knowing shit."

It's my turn to advance on him, and I do. I take steady, solid steps toward him, sliding my arm around his waist, backing him up against the edge of the bed.

"I don't like not knowing shit, either, Darren."

I don't miss the way his body melts, or the way his chest heaves with breath from my forced proximity.

He squirms beneath me and I push him back.

He falls against the bed easily, his gaze full of hunger.

"Will it... will it hurt?" he asks, his voice carrying an innocence his gaze does not.

I stop for a moment as I look at him, and something in his tone pulls my attention.

"I have studied your limits. I won't do anything you don't—"

"Oh no, not the punishment. I mean the... when..."

"English, Dare."

"I've never... bottomed before," he says, his cheeks reddening. "I should've noted that on the form, but there wasn't a *preference,* and—"

Somehow, this doesn't surprise me.

It also sparks intrigue, but at the moment, I cannot focus on my desires, or my punishments.

I need to *care* for Dare, and that means putting his needs above my own.

"Yes," I say as I turn to my duffel, knowing exactly what I need for this lesson. "But if you are prepared enough, trained enough, it won't hurt as much."

"Trained?" he asks, his voice darkening just a hair.

I find my tools and stalk closer to him, laying them out on the bed next to me.

"Take off your pants, now," I order.

Dare looks up at me, and I can see him debating whether or not to listen.

But thankfully, he does.

The sight of him naked before me, his thick, pink cock bobbing in the air, glistening with precum, tells me this is going to be a most enjoyable lesson.

"Yes, my little wild star. I told you, your body is capable of great things." I squeeze some cold lubricant onto my fingers.

Dare's pupils dilate again as he watches me, full understanding befalling him.

"Say it," I order.

I watch his lips part, his chest heave, making the wings of his tattoo dance over his nipples.

"M... my..." The strain in his voice is evident as his cock twitches.

"Say it, Dare."

"My body is capable of great things," he repeats, his voice loud and clear.

I push his legs open, wasting no time as I take him into my mouth, which causes him to groan and nearly jump off the bed.

"Oh fuck," he yelps.

His hands find my hair, and when I know he's good and distracted, I start to massage and rub his entrance, in the same torturous way he did to me a week ago.

"Oh my God," his voice catches as I slowly tease his entrance, making him curse, and only then, do I slide my finger in his tight hole.

"Fucking hell... I"

"You will not come," I tell him with sternness.

"Matty..." he whines.

"Not until I tell you, you can. Do you understand?"

His groan is full of frustration, and I take him to the back of my throat, just so I can hear it again.

"I can't, oh my God, I can't..."

"You will," I say matter of factly as I remove my finger and my mouth from him.

His body heaves with every breath.

I pour some more lubricant in my hand, making sure to get my fingers slick.

I slide the first back in with ease, and his moans make my own cock twitch.

I force myself to pay attention to *him* and not my own cock.

After all, I need to be in control, and I need to set a prime example.

"If it's too much, use your safe word," I remind him. "And I will stop."

Dare breathes heavily, but he says nothing.

I continue.

"You torment me, Dare. Edging me, baiting me, ignoring me..." My voice is dark yet eloquent as I lick the fresh bead of precum from his tip.

"And for that, you will be punished, so you learn your lesson." I slowly thrust my fingers inside of him, watching as he wriggles, listening as he curses up a storm.

"Fucking please... I want..."

"I know what you want," I assure him as I increase my rhythm before removing my fingers completely only to hear him swear again.

"It's not so fun when you're the one being played with, is it, Dare?"

Dare only whines as he moves to grab himself, but I stop him with a swift hand.

"No, no, no. You are going to learn your lesson."

"I am so going to get you back for this," he swears.

I can't help the grin that forms on my face.

"Just for that, I'm going to use the plug."

"The what?" He yelps, leaning up on his elbows.

It takes me hardly any time to lubricate the small silicone stopper.

"I promise it will only hurt for a moment." I watch his eyes glisten.

I have to fight to adjust my own cock, but I don't miss Dare's gaze as he looks at the noticeable bulge, knowing what he does to me.

I settle between his legs once more, taking my time as I tease and taunt his hole, if only to let him get used to the feel of it.

His cock weeps with arousal, and his breath is rapid. I know he's close.

"Please, Matty..." he begs, and the sound is like music to my ears.

"Please what, Dare?" I have him exactly where I want him.

"Please, let me come... please, please, please..."

"Oh, I don't know..." I taunt him, enjoying the sight of him wriggling beneath my touch, of his cock glistening in the light.

Dare whines again, and I slide the plug in completely.

He cries out with a groan that makes my own cock strain against my pants. I can feel a fresh bead of precum forming at my head and I know if I am not careful I, too, will come.

Because the sight of him like this is absolutely *perfect.*

He was made to be *mine.*

His body takes the plug easily, squeezing of its own accord.

"Promise you will do as I say?" I lick him from base to head.

"I promise," he whines. "Please, just let me come."

The whimper in his voice tells me he is close to breaking and I need to pull back.

So, I do.

"That's a good boy. Come for me, now, my little wild star."

The moment I take him into my mouth and pull the plug out, he breaks.

His hot release fills my mouth, and he lets out a string of curses and words that make no sense at all as I swallow him down like a cold glass of water.

When I'm finished, I gaze down at him, at the look of utter bliss on his face.

I set to cleaning him up, and he murmurs something I can't quite hear.

"What was that?" I ask.

He breathes deep, then says, "I love you."

Time stops.

And once again the ghosts I had long buried threaten to become tangible once again.

The desire to respond, to tell him, I love him, too, is paralyzing.

"Matty..." His voice is small, hesitant.

"You should eat something and get some rest," I reply.

Dare sits up on his elbows, the covers falling from him to expose the sight of of his stitched up heart tattoo.

Can you stitch me back together, Darren?

Can I let you?

"It's late, and we have a big day tomorrow."

I watch as he frowns, as the excitement in his eyes disappears.

Because of me.

"Okay," he says calmly.

"Good night, Darren." I say as I gather myself, and my broken parts.

And only when I have returned to the solace of my own sanctum, do I let go.

CHAPTER 23

Dare

I really am the worst boyfriend ever.

Though, I guess we've never really discussed our label, I checked the box for relationship preference as monogamous.

So that makes Matty my boyfriend, right?

I don't want anyone but him, anyway. Not now, and probably not ever. Because even if he changed his mind tomorrow and ripped up our contract, I know I'll never get over him.

His voice, his snarky attitude, the genius of his music, the way he can play me like a damn fiddle.

I hadn't *meant* to say the l word, but I can't deny the truth, either.

I do love Mateo Starr.

And I may have just fucked everything up. Again.

I chew on my cheese pizza in between bouts of writing. A knock on my door alerts me, and for a moment, I think maybe he's changed his mind.

That he'll come storming back in here and he'll tell me he loves me, too, and we can live happily ever after like in those Hallmark movies my mom's obsessed with.

I all but run to the door, opening it to see it's only Richie.

"Hey, everything okay?" he asks, and I can see he looks a little disheveled himself. His eyes are glassy and I realize he's upset.

Shit.

"What happened?" I ask as I pull him into my room.

He puts on a good front, but I can see he's clearly messed up.

And a little drunk.

"I fucked up," he says.

"What, how—"

"I might've told Hailee I loved her."

"Fuck, is this shit genetic or something?" I breathe in exasperation as he attempts to sit on the bed.

The bed where Matty was just—

"Don't sit there," I say, shaking my head.

"What, why?" he asks, then immediately his eyebrows shoot up.

"Oh my God, Dare!" He yelps as he jumps up.

"Oh, like you've never hooked up in a hotel room before," I bite.

Richie purses his lips. "Who was it?" he asks.

"Richie..." I back away from him.

"Who was it... Was it someone we know?"

I don't know why I tell him. Maybe because if I truly have fucked everything up, at least I'll have an ally.

Someone to help put me back together.

"It's Matty."

Richie's eyes widen. "Mateo? You're banging Hailee's *brother*?"

"No!" I defend hurriedly. "Well, not yet, anyway. I mean, like, it's a little more complicated than that."

God, now I sound like Matty.

Richie busts out laughing. "Shit, is there something in the fucking water?"

He slumps down on the floor and I bring the pizza with me, plopping it between us.

"Eat some pizza, man, it'll make you feel better."

He doesn't argue, only grabs a slice.

"So, I guess Hailee didn't say it back?"

Riche sighs. "No, she did."

"Then what's the problem?"

At least she said it back!

"I just... I'm not good at this sort of thing, you know."

"What sort of thing?" I ask, pulling some melted cheese off my slice.

"The whole relationship thing. Like, I know I'm twenty-six and I'm not, like, young, by any means, but..."

"Maybe you should make a contract," I say.

"What?" Richie looks at me in horror.

"Never mind," I reply, shoving my face with some more pizza to hide my embarrassment.

"What about you?" he asks. "You said it was genetic. You tell Mateo you love him too or something?"

"Maybe." I don't look at him because I can't.

"And I guess he didn't say it back?"

I shake my head. "I mean, I kinda dropped it like a bombshell in the middle of—"

"Oh my God!" Richie smacks me. "Did you mean it?"

I bite my lip, nodding. "Yeah. But I think I scared him."

Richie gives me a half smile. "We're a fucking mess, aren't we?" he says, his voice slightly slurred.

"Yeah, we kind of are."

Richie pulls another piece of pizza from the box.

"Well, if we're gonna both be messes, at least we're hot ones," he says seriously, and I can't help but bust out laughing.

Richie laughs, too.

"More like hot shit on a burning sidewalk," I say as I shove him.

And for the first time in a long time, I feel like Richie gets more than I think he does.

AFTER A LONG DAY OF SIGHTSEEING, press,

and rehearsal, I'm more than happy to crash in my hotel room.

My phone rings, and I debate shutting off the ringer entirely, but on the odd chance Matty might actually text me, I don't want to miss him.

So, I grab the phone, answering it if only to bitch at whatever extended car warranty assholes I have to to stop calling me, when I recognize the number as my Doctor back in LA.

I breathe a sigh of relief as they read me my results. I've never been good at tests, and this might be the only one I passed with flying colors.

And probably the only one that really matters.

I lean back on my bed, letting my exhaustion and my relief take hold.

WHEN I WAKE UP, it's to the sound of a knock on my door.

One glance at the clock, and I note it's barely nine thirty, which means I've been out for nearly two hours.

I rub my eyes as I head to the door, opening it to see Matty.

Dressed in his usual funeral attire, with a literal bouquet of roses.

Black roses, to be exact.

"What the?"

"I'm sorry," he says the words definitively.

"For what?" I ask, feeling like the air has been sucked out of my lungs.

"Can I come in?" he asks, his voice like velvet.

It's not commanding, demanding, or stern.

It's *hopeful.*

I can't help but nod, appreciating the sight of him looking absolutely perfect with a bunch of flowers.

For me.

I step aside as he enters, closing the door softly behind him.

He hands me the flowers, and I watch as his expression shifts to one of guilt.

"I'm sorry for... a lot of things. I haven't been the best..."

I watch him sigh, his shoulders sinking.

I don't want to tear my eyes away from him, but the flowers are fucking pretty.

A closer look shows the edges of the petals are crimson red.

"Boyfriend?" I test the word in the air.

Matty purses his lips.

"I mean, you really should, like, clarify that on the form."

I watch as he pulls a folded up piece of paper out of his back pocket. He grips it tightly, and I can see his jaw tense.

"He cheated on me," he says slowly. "Even though he checked monogamous."

His words are full of pain, and I can't help but set the flowers down and take a step toward him.

Matty stares at the paper in his hand, and I feel like he's about to have a mental breakdown or something.

I only took one semester of Psychology, damn it!

I am not equipped for this!

"He stopped returning my texts. So, I followed the rules of the contract and—"

"Shit," I say, feeling like the worse boyfriend on the planet.

"Matty, I'm sorry. I—" I watch as he stills, gazing down at me with determination.

"Before I met you, I thought I knew what I needed. Order, structure. The chance to *care* for someone, in the only way I know how." He licks his lips, and I am powerless to move.

"I thought being in control of my emotions meant I couldn't be hurt. That compartmentalizing things was what was best. I didn't even *miss* being touched."

He opens the paper, and hands it to me.

"What is this?" I ask as I take it from him.

"Me," he says softly, his voice barely a whisper.

I look down at the paper. The form is familiar, a spot for a name, a section to tick off relationship preference. Everything looks the same until I get to the part about the roles.

When I signed my contract, I'd noted the box for "switch/vers" only because I was unsure of what I wanted at the time, and I figured exploring both sides might be fun.

But Matty hasn't checked that box, or the one I expected he would.

My heart pounds in my chest like a drum as the air around me thins.

Matty's checked submissive.

I glance up at him, to see him standing, perfectly still, his hands behind his back, and it's at that moment, I notice his shoulders are *relaxed.*

"My test results are in there, too. Clean slate, of course."

"Matty..." My voice is but a whisper.

I watch as he shifts his weight.

"My safeword is Icarus," he says calmly. He nods at the paper in my hand.

I flip the papers, glancing at his limits.

My gaze dips to his preferences. Orgasm denial, bondage, and a few others that I can barely read because the weight of the situation has my vision blurring.

Tears beg to be freed.

"My results came in, too. Clean slate, of course," I say as I try not to crumble into a million pieces as I fight to speak.

Matty's expression is stoic as I flip to the last page.

"I thought what I needed was order. Structure. Control," he says. "But what I really needed, Dare... was you."

He takes one small step to close the distance between us. "Say something," he whispers.

"I love you, Mateo," I say, my voice thick

with emotion. I grab his face in my hands, and I pull him to me, coveting his lips with my own.

Mateo Star doesn't fight me. He only wraps his arms around my waist and holds me like he's afraid I'll disappear.

When he breaks apart from our kiss, his gravelly voice sings.

"You are infinity, a fire burning bright in the darkness, shining through space and time. My black hole, my supernova, my wild, wild star... and you are mine."

CHAPTER 24

Matty

I'VE NEVER FELT SO EXPOSED in all my life.

Dare kisses me with a passion that could be described as nothing short of a supernova.

"I want *you*," I whisper, needing him to understand the depth of my submission. I settle my hand over his chest over his stitched up heart.

For the briefest moment, there is a pause, and I think he's going to safeword out.

That this, that *I* am too much for him.

That I've just scared the shit out of him.

He sucks in a deep breath, flashing his gaze up at me from beneath his dark lashes.

"I want..." He pauses, biting his bottom lip. "To see you naked, on that bed with your cock wet and ready for me." Then he whispers, "Sir."

I can't help the grin that spreads on my face as he starts to ramble.

"Or, like, wait... if you're, like, my submissive... do you prefer slut? Whore? Is there some other term I should know that—"

I waste no time removing my clothes, keeping my gaze trained on him as I find my way to the bed.

I watch as his eyes widen, and he grabs himself while he stares at me the same way he did at Saint & Sinner when he was on that stage.

Like I am *everything* he's ever wanted.

The feeling is mutual, sir.

Dare shimmies out of his sweatpants as he comes to stand at the edge of the bed.

"I want to watch you come," he says, the familiar aura of dominance surfacing in him once more. "Like a... like a good little *cockslut.*"

I smirk, because watching him explore this side of himself, like this... comfortable, confident... it's the sexiest thing I've ever seen.

His cock springs free as he takes it in his hand, slowly stroking.

I slowly start to pull and stroke my cock, spreading my precum as it beads at the tip. My voice is clear as a bell when I say, "Yes, sir."

Dare grins, kneeling on the bed, and it dips from his weight, making me slink a little further down.

My gaze is fixed on his cock, and I can't help but think about how *good* it would feel buried to the hilt inside of me.

It's been a long time since I let anyone fuck me, but the reality that I want Dare to do so is as monumental as my confession.

This man who kills me, who tears me apart only to stitch me back together again.

My wild star.

We blur together like stars in the sky.

Dare looms over me once more, taking my lips with his as he thrusts his cock against mine.

I wrap my legs around his hips, pulling him closer.

"Is this what you want, Matty?" he growls, thrusting his cock against mine as he torments my entrance with the edge of his thumb again.

I will not come this easily, this soon.

I have trained for this!

"Maybe," I breathe.

The intrusion of his finger is startling, but it feels good. But it's not enough.

"Tell me what you want," he says, sliding another finger in to stretch me, and I know this isn't just love.

It's punishment.

A deep groan escapes my lips as I submit to his whim.

He brings me to the edge, not once, not twice, but four times before I am so wound up, I think I may actually spontaneously combust.

"Ready to tap out yet, Matty?" he taunts me.

"No, sir." I huff in frustration. "I can take it."

Dare grunts, "You think you can take me, huh?" He removes his fingers, sliding between my legs in one swift motion.

The moment his tongue laps at me, I cry out.

"Yes," I grunt.

"I want to hear you say it," he says, tormenting me.

And for the first time in a long time, I don't feel scared of the words. I am emboldened by them.

"I want you to fuck me until I come all over you. Sir," I say with the utmost confidence.

"Oh, fuck me," Dare curses as he kisses me, before reaching to the nightstand table.

"You're not ready yet, baby," I remind him, breaking character, if only for a moment.

Dare shakes his head, his gaze full of fire as I watch him squirt a hefty amount of lube into his hand, watching as he smoothes it over his thickness.

"Mhmm. We'll see who's ready." He smirks, his tone full of that bratty attitude I favor so much as he angles himself over me once more.

The weight of him against me is heavenly, and I find myself getting lost in the galaxy within his eyes.

A couple slow pumps of his fingers bring me back to the here and now as he looks at me with glistening eyes.

"Are you sure?" he asks, softly, breaking character.

I think maybe he's going to tap out.

I nod. "Yes, sir. I'm sure."

The moment our bodies connect, it's astronomical.

Nothing, and no one has ever felt this *good*.

Dare inches himself in, the movement torturously slow, and I think I'm not the only one in danger of losing control.

I hook my legs around his hips, pulling him closer, finding his lips with my own.

All the chaos dies as we find our rhythm together.

The chase is maddening, but the love...

The love I feel from the way he kisses me, touches me, his slow, relaxed thrusts... that love buries itself within me, until it is all I know.

"Come for me," Dare whispers against my lips hungrily. "Please."

The desperation in his voice is my undoing.

I grin wickedly as I slide my hand between us, finding his wet, warm cock. The tides shift between us once more.

"Come *with* me," I whisper as I lose control, kissing him with all that I am.

Dare groans into my mouth, and then I feel him in every part of my being.

And as we both reach the heavens together, like perfectly aligned satellites, I realize I am finally *home.*

CHAPTER 25

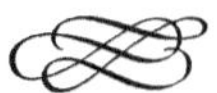

DARE

MATTY BURIES his face in my shoulder, groaning in his sleep as my alarm sounds like a damn foghorn.

"Fucking shut that off," he grunts.

I try my hardest to reach the damn thing, but with Mateo Star holding onto me like a damn koala on a eucalyptus tree, I have to *stretch.*

Which knocks my damn phone off the night-stand, onto the floor, and shuts it off for the time being.

"I think I'm losing circulation in my arm," I

quip, but my voice is full of laughter, and I can't stop smiling.

Matty threads his leg through mine, nuzzling his lips against my neck.

"Bullshit," he groans, his gravelly Batman voice so much sexier when he's half awake.

His cock presses against my side and the memories come rushing back.

The roses still sit on the dresser, the only evidence that what happened... really fucking *happened.*

Matty showed up at my door and told me he loved me.

He gave me his heart in ink and flesh, and I gave him the same.

"What time is it, anyway?" he asks as he pulls me closer, planting a kiss on my lips.

"Like eight thirty, why?"

"I told Geo and Hailee I'd meet them for brunch at eleven."

"Eleven? That seems kinda late."

"What can I say, I like to sleep in when I can," he says with a grin, hooking his knuckle under my chin.

"This is not sleeping," I say as I sink into his kiss.

He thrusts his hardness against me and I can't help the moan that escapes my throat.

I am at his fucking mercy, and I don't think that will ever change.

"Sure it is," he whispers darkly.

The alarm blares once more and we both groan.

"I'm heading for the shower," I say, jumping from the bed and heading for the bathroom. I turn to see Matty dressing himself, but his dark hair looks disheveled as hell, and despite his nice clothes, there is no denying the truth of the matter.

Sex hair does not lie.

"I'll see you at the show then," he says, clearing his throat as he stops in front of me.

I'm acutely aware of my nakedness, but I don't give a shit for once.

When Matty looks at me, I feel like a star.

"Yeah. I'll see you then," I reply as he leans in to place the softest kiss on my lips.

"Stay out of trouble, okay?" he says, but his tone is light.

"I make no promises."

And that's the damn truth.

I WATCH as Matty and Hailee finish up their last song. *Satellites.* The crowd roars, calling for an encore, and I can't help but smile.

Matty's gaze flashes to mine and I give him a knowing look. The crowd chants, and that's when I hear their words, or *word*, I should say.

Control.

A smile forms on my face and I give him the thumbs up.

He looks at Hailee, who is not moving, poised at her keyboard. And that's when I see the familiar mess of blond hair on the opposite side of the stage. I wave to my brother, but he doesn't see me.

He's too fixed on Hailee.

Matty speaks into his microphone. "You want control, huh?" he asks, his dark, gravelly voice causing a sea of screams to erupt.

I holler from the sidelines.

"What do you think, Hailee? Think we should give them *control*?"

Hailee nods, grinning as she speaks into her microphone. "Oh, fuck yeah!" she replies and the crowd screams again.

Matty strums the chords on his guitar, looks at her, and then stops.

"You know... I could use a little back up, though." He nods to Hailee.

"Hmmm, you might be onto something," she chirps, flashing him with a grin. "Like, what if we had a *killer* bassist." Her eyes sparkle with evil intent.

"Oh no," I say to myself as Richie stands straighter.

"Yeah, and maybe a *killer* guitarist to back up my vocals."

The crowd screams.

"Yeah, I think we have some *killer* musicians who could help us out." Hailee smiles before heading into the wings, and Matty turns to look at me, smirking like the absolute asshole he is.

"What do you say, *Dare*? You got any more juice?" His grin is wicked, and I shake my head.

Fucking hell. I'm going to make him pay for this later.

And I'm going to enjoy the hell out of it, too.

I don't think twice about strolling out on stage. After all, it's where I've always felt the most comfortable.

And sharing a stage with the man I love... well, that's just a fucking bonus.

A stagehand hands me a mic clip as Hailee pulls my brother on stage.

It takes both of us all of two minutes to get our instruments and sound packs, and get in place.

I stand behind Matty, my gaze catching his as he nods.

"Knock 'em dead, wild star."

"Yes, sir," I reply as I strum out the beginning chords of *Control*, finally feeling like all my dreams have finally come true.

EPILOGUE

THREE WEEKS LATER
Dare

"YOU HEAR BACK YET about the song?" Matty asks, carrying down my bags from my tour bus, loading them onto the luggage racks for the hotel.

"No, not yet, but I did just submit it yesterday," I remind him.

He shrugs. "Still, I think if they don't like it, you should release it on your own. Put it on your YouTube or something."

It's my turn to raise an eyebrow as I sling my backpack over my shoulder.

"Maybe. But I'm not worried about it. I know it's good. Because *we* wrote it."

Matty lets out a sigh. "I told you, you didn't have to credit me. It's *your* song."

"Yeah, and you helped. Thus credit," I repy as I take the lead.

Richie and the rest of the band *loved* the final cut of *Wild Star*, and after only a few days on the road, we'd written a damn good hook, and managed to cut the song pretty clean.

I know it is different than anything else we've done, after all, *Heart Killer* isn't the type to do power ballads to begin with, but I think it's got a lot of potential.

I think it would make one hell of a next single.

But right now, the only reason I'm even talking about the damn thing, is so that I can keep Matty's attention span on *anything* else, because I feel like I'm going to explode from holding on to this fucking secret right now.

"I have reservations for us at the restaurant. Figured you wouldn't mind too much. I know you get fucking bitchy if you don't stick to your routine," I taunt him.

Matty hip checks me, nearly knocking me and my backpack over.

"Yeah, and you get bitchy without your damn rice crispy treats. Those things are terrible for you, you know."

"You know what else is bad for me? You. On an empty stomach," I bite out.

"When you have a black balloon birthday, Dare, you'll understand."

I roll my eyes.

"So fucking dramatic. You're forty, not a hundred."

"I am one year closer to death," he nips.

"Still sexy, though," I declare, trying to appear flirtatious and not like I'm harboring knowledge that in t-minus five minutes I'll be dropping Mateo Starr into a room full of rockstars. With cake.

Matty shakes his head as he commands me to drop off my shit, but his bark is worse than his bite.

Regardless, I drop off my bags to the bellhop while Matty checks us in, texting Hailee and my brother to let her know we've arrived.

"I'm fucking starving," he groans as he slips

his hand around my waist. "I could really use a good glass of whiskey and a nice, juicy steak."

"Uh huh," I reply as I lead us around the bend to the restaurant, giving the host my name, knowing in just a matter of moments, Matty will probably have plenty more reasons to punish me.

The host opens the door, and the moment Matty steps in, the resounding hollers of *surprise* and *happy birthday* ring out in tandem.

His eyes widen as he turns to me, jaw tense. "You—"

"Are going to pay for this later? Yeah, I know." I chuckle nervously as Hailee comes up and throws her arms around her brother.

Richie waves to me, grinning from ear to ear.

"Happy Birthday, Mateo!" Hailee says sweetly as she kisses him on the cheek.

"It is a very merry *un-birthday*, but thank you."

Geo comes up next to us, clapping his friend on the back. "You're only as old as you feel, right?"

Matty grumbles, shooting me a scathing glare. "Yes, well, that's easy for all of you to say, you're not the oldest one here."

"Technically, *Duncan* is the oldest one here,"

Felix's voice makes me turn around, along with Matty.

Felix grins as Duncan extends his hand to Matty.

"You know dating someone over a decade younger than you will age you faster, right?" he says with a laugh.

I can't help but laugh as Felix shoots him a dramatic look.

"How dare you," he says, his mock-shock quite funny.

Duncan laughs, and his entire body moves with it. "It's true!"

"Unbelievable," Felix says, turning back to us.

"Perhaps you two can start a club," he says bitterly, as Richie calls out, "Cake's here!"

"Finally!" I exclaim with excitement as I leave my boyfriend and the rest of the awkward as fuck conversation in favor of my favorite thing.

Dessert.

When Richie lights the candle on Matty's cupcake, I lead the choir.

Matty tries not to smile, but he fails miserably.

"All right, Batman, make a wish," I say as I

present him with a single cupcake with one candle.

Matty takes it from my hands, his smile so genuine behind the flame, that it makes me respond in unison.

"I already have everything I could ever want." His voice is dark, sultry, and I can't fight my blush.

He holds the cupcake in front of me. "Blow," he says, flashing me with a smirk.

"Yes, sir," I whisper as I make my own wish, watching the flame go out.

Everyone cheers and I pull out the candle, licking the icing off.

Matty sets his cupcake down on the table next to us, stealing my candle from between my fingers, taking one step toward me.

In that one step, he manages to push me back up against the table, and I have to brace myself.

He reaches out, wiping some icing from my mouth, and I think I'll never get over moments like this.

Ever.

"What did you wish for, wild star?" he purrs.

"I'm not telling," I say darkly.

"I have ways of making you talk," he says as

he kisses me, licking the bottom of my lip, and I feel more on display than ever in this room full of people, with Matty *licking* me.

I gaze up at him, and I forget about all of them.

All there is, is this.

Us.

"That's what I'm counting on."

Three Weeks Later
Mateo

"And that was *Heart Killer* with their newest single, *Wild Star*!"

I can't help but smile, feeling a sense of pride over the success my boyfriend's latest single is picking up. It debuted at number one, knocking *Satellites* to number two, and I couldn't be happier to be considered second.

I steal a glance at Dare, who's curled up next to the window in the backseat next to his brother, while Hailee is absentmindedly scrolling her phone.

"Are we there yet?" Dare groans from the backseat, like the little brat he is.

"Almost," I reply.

It's been nearly six weeks since we started this tour. And due to unforeseen circumstances, our original venue in Tucson was changed for the next show, so we've all got a few extra days to soak up the Arizona sun.

Which is how Hailee roped us all into this trip to the Grand Canyon today, including Geo and his friend, Zeb... which I'm actually looking forward to.

I know this new *demographic,* as he calls it, is quite new for him, but I'd be lying if I said I wasn't interested in meeting the man that has Geo so... bubbly.

"This place better have somewhere decent to eat because I'm damn starving," Hailee says.

"Me too," Dare whines in the back.

I can't help but shake my head. "You know it's the middle of nowhere, right?"

"They have to have a food truck or something!" Dare growls.

I sigh, knowing arguing with him is a lost cause.

When we finally arrive, Geo and his friend

are not there. I shoot them off a text, and sure enough, Geo tells me they stopped at some dive bar on the way up for something to eat.

I don't know much about what caused the rift between Geo and his former bandmate, except for the basics of what Geo's told me. That Zeb was his guitarist, and that Geo had pursued Casualty on his own, apart from his former partner.

But that's typical in this line of work. Bands, singers... the players are always changing.

Even those of us who think they'll *never* change.

Like when you perform with one person for twenty years and think you'll never collaborate... only to discover you can work with other people.

And the experience is *fun.*

Which is how I ended up getting roped into playing guitar when Dare performs *Wild Star* now at our shows.

Not long after our conversation, I note the candy apple red pickup truck flying into the private tours parking lot.

When Geo and his *friend* get out of the car, I notice the smile on his face immediately.

He looks *happy.* Happier than I think I've seen him in the last ten years.

"Hey, G!" My sister squeals with excitement as she runs up and hugs him.

Richie also pulls him in for a friendly hug while Dare slaps him on the back, and I don't miss how Zeb stands frozen, staring at them like glaciers in the middle of the desert.

"Hi! I'm Dare!" Dare chirps happily as he approaches the dark-haired, beastly looking man. I'd seen him when we arrived, picking up Geo from the hotel, but that was from afar. Up close, I can get a good look at him.

He's tall, almost as tall as me, with a deep, rich tan that can only come from being a native to the area. Combined with his sturdy build, medium length dark hair and beard, he looks like he could pass for a bit older than twenty-nine.

"Nice to meet you, Dare," he replies with a polite grin, but I note the way his shoulders are tense, even as he shakes my boyfriend's hand. He's nervous.

Interesting.

"This is my boyfriend, Matty!" Dare says as he practically shoves me toward the man to make an introduction.

Zeb glances at me, sizing me up. I want to smirk, because the aura of protectiveness rolling off of him tells me everything I need to know about how he feels about my friend, even if he doesn't say it out loud.

"It's Mateo," I advise him, sliding an arm around Dare and pulling him closer.

Hailee hugs him, and I steal a look at Geo. He looks like a kid on Christmas morning, smiling from ear to ear with excitement.

"This is Zebulon, my—" Geo's voice disappears and then there is a miniscule silence as he looks to his *demographic*, who only responds with, "friend."

Geo frowns only slightly, but soon recovers, even if it is not genuine.

Perhaps Geo is not the only one wading into unknown waters.

Something tells me this Zebulon may be encountering new challenges of his own.

When we finally arrive at the canyon, Dare is the first to plop his sweet ass down on the ground.

With his space cat tank top and his long, dark hair pulled back into a bun, long eyelashes standing out against the desert orange tones surrounding us, he looks absolutely perfect.

I take a seat next to him, removing a bottle of water and a rice crispy treat from my backpack.

"Thought you might need this." I offer him the items.

"You're a fucking angel," he groans, tearing the treat right out of my hand.

In my peripheral vision, I can see Geo and Zeb standing beside one another, talking closely. Richie and Hailee are snapping a million selfies of themselves with the dessert.

I'm sure their photo will be everywhere the second it hits Instagram.

"You know that stuff is terrible for you, right?" I open my own water.

Dare tears into his rice crispy treat, moaning like he does when I have him tied up in my Italian ropes.

"Sugar makes everything better," he gushes, licking his fingers clean.

"Spice is quite nice, too," I say, pulling out my own snack; some gochujang seaweed crisps.

"Bet the stars here would be fucking top tier," he says softly through bouts of chewing.

I wrap my arms around him, a smile

forming on my face. His body is warm and sweaty, and fits to my side perfectly. Like the sun and the moon fit together for an eclipse, existing as something rare, beautiful, and magical.

"Maybe we'll have to come back and see for ourselves," I suggest, looking down at his fiery, dark eyes. Dare looks up at me, and I think there is no better sight. Grand Canyon or not.

The smile that forms on his face is sublime.

"Hmmm... that gives me an idea..." He flashes me with a mischievous grin.

"Good idea or bad idea?" I ask, because with Dare, I never know how things will end up.

But if I'm being honest, that's why I love him.

"I'll let you be the judge," he says as he leans his head on my shoulder.

"Yes, sir," I reply as I hold him close, singing out the melody of my current work in progress, *Savior.*

"Rescue me from anarchy, deliver me from war

Show me what it's like to love, my savior

And I'll show you what it's like to be adored."

Dare swoons at my voice, and I grin.

When he sings along, improvising lyrics of his own, I think there's nothing better than this.

The music we make.

Together.

Just me, and my savior, my little wild star.

"I'll slay the dragons, I'll bring you the moon

I'm a *Heart Killer*, Matty, and I fucking love you,"* Dare sings, his tone full of that bratty bravado I can't get enough of.

"You are certifiable," I whisper as I tilt his chin up, brushing my thumb over his bottom lip. I kiss him, losing myself in his sweet chaos once more, letting my hand fall to his neck, squeezing lightly.

The motion draws out a sweet groan from his mouth, so I do it again.

I don't think I'll ever get over the sounds he makes for me.

They are like music to my ears.

When we break apart, he settles back against me, wrapping his arm around my back and cuddling close to me, the both of us silent as we take in the beauty of our surroundings, together, in perfect harmony.

Thank you for reading Wild Stars!
Continue with the next book in the Rock His
World series, Grave Misgivings.

IF YOU ENJOYED THIS BOOK, maybe you'll do me a huge favor and leave a review. Even a few words would mean the world to me, and it also helps other readers find the stories you love.

THANKS!
~*Evie Riley*

Rock His World

Hollow Heart

Wild Stars

Grave Misgivings

Federal Protection Agency

Mason

Rafe

Ryzen

Cooper

Noah

Damien

Sebastian

Gabe

Logan

Ruthless Empire

Courting Danger

Chasing Danger

Kissing Danger

Smokejumpers

Hawke

Cyrus

Jase

Gage

Jackson

Xavier

Jasper Springs

Cade

Dawson

Drew

Grayson

Riley

Mitch

From The Edge

Shattered

Runaway

Jaded

Rescue

Hidden

Tormented

Gray Vale Pack

His Fated Mate

His Wounded Warrior

His Healing Heart

Evie Riley is a prolific, neurodivergent author known for her captivating MM romance novels. She has gained a significant following and topped the LGBT+ action and adventure bestseller charts with her series.

Evie's writing style often explores dark and gritty themes where her men must overcome difficult obstacles in their search for love, but she has also ventured into sweeter small-town romances, incorporating tropes like enemies-to-lovers, friends-to-lovers, age-gap, and forced proximity. She is known for crafting engaging romantic suspense novels and has a knack for creating interconnected series worlds that keep readers invested.

Outside of writing, she enjoys spending time at the beach and has a quirky personality, described by her partner as ranging from cute to deadly, depending on her blood-chocolate levels.

Evie spends her nights writing bad boys in love, and her days wrangling the sweet boys she loves.